FROM DIRT
TO DIAMONDS

FROM DIRT TO DIAMONDS

BY

JULIA JAMES

MILLS & BOON

First published in Great Britain 2011
by Mills & Boon, an imprint of Harlequin (UK) Limited.
Large Print edition 2011
Harlequin (UK) Limited, Eton House,
18-24 Paradise Road, Richmond, Surrey TW9 1SR

© Julia James 2011

ISBN: 978 0 263 22249 4

Harlequin (UK) policy is to use papers that are natural, renewable and recyclable products and made from wood grown in sustainable forests. The logging and manufacturing process conform to the legal environmental regulations of the country of origin.

Printed and bound in Great Britain
by CPI Antony Rowe, Chippenham, Wiltshire

CHAPTER ONE

ANGELOS PETRAKOS eased his broad shoulders in the wide-backed dining chair and reached a long-fingered hand for his wineglass. He took a mouthful of the extremely expensive vintage, savouring it. His glance flicked around the crowded, fashionable Knightsbridge restaurant, momentarily diverted from his host, with whom he was in discussion about a particular joint venture with Petrakos International.

Immediately he was aware of female eyes assessing him.

A mordant look gave a dark glint to his obsidian eyes. How much of their interest was in him and how much in his position as head of a multinational conglomerate with a range of businesses in its highly profitable portfolio?

It was a distinction his widowed father had been incapable of making. So astute in business, in building the Petrakos empire, yet his father had been targeted by one financially predatory female after another, and the youthful Angelos had been repelled by it. He'd hated to see his vulnerable father exploited, lured into loaning them money, making investments in their business affairs, or promoting their careers with his wealth and contacts. Angelos had learnt his lesson well, and so, however alluring the woman, however tempting it was to have an affair with her, he was ruthless in keeping business and pleasure scrupulously separate.

Such self-control could be irksome, but his rule was inflexible and absolute—he never allowed any beautiful and ambitious woman to take advantage of his interest in them. It was simpler and safer that way.

His gaze continued its swift sweep of the restaurant, ignoring the attempts to catch his eye, while his attention remained still attuned to what his host was saying about the complex financial structure of the deal he was proposing. Then, abruptly, his grip on his wineglass tightened. His gaze honed down between the heads of other diners to the far side of the room, to a table set against the opposite wall.

A woman, sitting in profile to him.

He stilled completely. Then slowly, very slowly,

he lowered his wineglass to the table. His gaze had not moved an iota. His eyes were hard as steel. For one long, measureless moment he held his gaze immobile. Then, abruptly cutting across whatever his host had been saying, he said, 'Excuse me one moment.' His voice was terse. As hard as his eyes.

He pushed back his chair, getting to his feet, discarding his napkin on the table. Then, with a lithe, powerful tread, he headed across the restaurant.

Towards his target.

Thea lifted her glass, smiling across at her dinner partner, and took a delicate sip of her flavoured mineral water. Even though Giles was enjoying a fine vintage Chablis, she never drank alcohol herself. It was not just empty calories—it was dangerous. For a second so brief she did not register it by time the flicker of a shadow feinted over her skin. Then Giles spoke, dispelling it.

'Thea...'

His voice was tentative. She smiled reassuringly, despite the nerves which ate her inside. *Please let him say it...*

She had worked so hard, so long for this

moment, and now what she hungered for so much was almost within her reach.

'Thea—' Giles said again, his voice sounding more determined now.

And again Thea found herself willing him to continue. *Please let him say it! Please!*

But even as the words begged in her head she saw him pause.

A shadow fell over the table.

It was curious, Angelos found himself thinking with an abstract part of his mind, just how swiftly he had recognised her. It had been, after all, nearly five years. Yet she had been instantly identifiable in the first second his eyes had lighted on her just now. The same abstract portion of his brain felt a flicker of emotion. He dispelled it swiftly.

Of course he had recognised her. He would know her anywhere. There could be no hiding place for her.

Now, as he reached the table she was sitting at, he could just what she had done to herself. It was, he acknowledged, remarkable. His gaze rested on her. Seeing, for the moment, what she wanted the world to see.

A stunningly beautiful female. A woman to catch the breath of any man.

But then she always had been that. But not like this. Not with sleek, pale, perfect hair—styled immaculately, drawn off her face into a sculpted chignon at the nape of her neck—her make-up so subtle that it was as if she were wearing none, the shimmer of pearls at her earlobes, her couture dress the colour of champagne in tailored silk, high-cut, long-sleeved.

Almost, he laughed. Harsh, unhumorous. To see her like this—chic, elegant, soignée… A thousand miles from the way she had once looked. Five long years from that. Five long years in which to create the transformation his outward eye now saw. The illusion.

More than an illusion. *A lie.*

His shadow fell across her. She turned her head. And in the one microsecond that it took he saw the shock—far more than shock!—detonate in her eyes. Then it was gone. Almost he admired her. Admired her for slamming down the visor over her face, the blankness—the flawless, perfect lack of any sign whatsoever of recognition, of acknowledgement of his identity.

But admiration was not what he felt for her. What he felt for her was—

Something different. Something quite, quite different. Something that had been buried deep for five long years. Crushed like rocks under lava that had once burnt blisteringly hot and which had cooled to impenetrable basalt.

Until this moment. Out of nowhere.

His hand slid inside the silk-lined inner breast pocket of his jacket, withdrawing a card. He flicked it down on to the table in front of her.

'Call me,' he said. His voice was expressionless. His face expressionless.

Then he turned and walked away.

As he did, he reached for his mobile phone, pressing a single number. Instantly it was answered.

'The blonde. I want a full dossier on her when I get back to my suite tonight.' He paused minutely. 'And her swain.'

Then he slid the phone away and rejoined his table. His face was still expressionless.

'My apologies,' he said smoothly to his host. 'You were saying…?'

'Thea? What on earth?' Giles's upper-class accents sounded bemused.

She lifted her eyes from the card. For a moment something seemed to move in her face.

'Angelos Petrakos.' She heard Giles read out the name on the card. It came from a long, long way away. Down an endless corridor of purgatory.

Angelos Petrakos. The name speared through her mind. *Five years. Five years—*

She could feel shock still detonating through her. Invisible, but explosive. A destructive force she could barely endure. But endure it she must—*must*. It was essential. Yet she felt as if a shockwave was slamming through her, convulsing her, and all she could do was hang on—hang on with her fingernails—as its force sought to overwhelm her.

In the wake of the shockwave came another devastating force—panic. A scorching, searing heat, screaming up in her chest, suffocating her. With an effort she could scarcely bear, she crushed down the shock, the panic. Regained control. Frail—paper-thin. But there all the same, holding everything down, pinning everything down.

I can do this!

The words, gritted out into the seething maelstrom in her head, were called up from the depths. Familiar words—words that had once been a litany. A litany that had somehow, *somehow*, got her through. Got her through to where she was now. In control. Safe.

She forced herself to blink, to focus on Giles's face. The face of the man who represented to her everything that she had ever craved, ever hungered for. And he was still there—still sitting opposite her. Still safe for her.

Everything's all right—it's still all right...

Urgently, she crushed down the panic in her throat.

Giles had turned his head to look at the tall figure striding across the restaurant. 'Not the type to bother with good manners,' he said, disapproval open in his voice.

Thea felt a bubble of hysteria bead dangerously in her throat, seeking to break through her rigid, desperate self-control.

Good manners? Good manners from Angelos Petrakos? A man whose last words to me five long bitter years ago had been to call me a—

He mind slammed shut. *No! Don't think. Don't remember—not for a single moment!*

Giles was talking again. She forced herself to listen, to keep crushed down the storming emotions ravaging inside her with sick, sick terror. To deny, utterly, what had just happened. That

Angelos Petrakos—the man who had destroyed her—had just surfaced out of nowhere, *nowhere*, like a dark, malignant demon…

Panic clawed again in her, its talons like slashing razors.

'Perhaps he wants to engage you,' Giles said, looking back across at her. 'Seems an odd way to go about it, though. Extremely uncivil. Anyway…' his voice changed, sounding awkward, self-conscious suddenly '…no need for you to accept any more bookings—well, that is if you— Well, if you—'

He cleared his throat.

'The thing is, Thea,' he resumed, 'what I was going to say before that chap interrupted was—well, would you consider—?'

He broke off again. Inside Thea the claws stopped abruptly. A stillness had formed. She couldn't move. Nor breathe.

For a moment Giles just looked at her—helpless, inarticulate. Then, with a lift of his chin, and in a voice that was suddenly not hesitant or inarticulate, but quiet and simple, he said, 'Would you, my dear Thea, consider doing me the very great honour of marrying me?'

She shut her eyes. Felt behind the lids tears stinging.

And everything that was storming in her brain—the shock, the panic, the terrified clinging of her fingernails to stop herself plunging down, down, down into the engulfing depths that she could feel trying to overwhelm her—suddenly, quite suddenly, ceased.

She opened her eyes. Gratitude streamed through her. Profound and seismic relief.

'Of course I will, Giles,' she answered, her voice soft and choked, the tears shimmering in her eyes like diamonds. Relief flooded through her. A relief so profound it felt like an ocean tide.

She was safe. Safe. For the first time in her life. And nothing, *no one*, could touch her now.

As the terror and panic drained out of her in the sweet, blessed relief of Giles's proposal, she almost twisted her head to spear her defiance across the room—to slay the one man in the world she had cause to loathe with all her being. But she wouldn't do it. She wouldn't give him the satisfaction of knowing that he even registered in her consciousness. Whatever malign quirk of fate had brought him here tonight, it had allowed him to witness—even if he had no idea it was happening!—a moment of supreme achievement in her life.

A hard sliver of satisfaction darted in her mind. All the shock and the panic she had felt were gone now—completely gone. Unneeded and unnecessary. Instead there was now thin, vicious satisfaction. It was fitting—oh, so fitting!—that he should be here, in the moment of her life's grateful achievement, when he had nearly, so very nearly, destroyed her life.

But I wouldn't let him! I clawed my way back and now I'm here, and I've got everything I've wanted all my life! So go to hell, Angelos Petrakos! Get out of my life and stay out for ever!

Then, casting him away with her damnation, she gazed into Giles's eyes. The eyes of the man she was going to marry.

On the far side of the room Angelos Petrakos's eyes were bladed like knives.

The rest of the evening passed in a blur for Thea. Gratitude and relief were paramount, but she also knew that there were still grave difficulties ahead of her. She was not—how could she be?—the ideal bride for Giles. But she knew how hard she would work to succeed as his wife—a wife he would never regret marrying, that even his parents would accept as well. She would not let them down. Nor Giles. For what he was giving her was beyond price to her. And she would not risk him regretting it.

And I can do it! I remade myself out of what I was—and I can make myself a suitable wife for Giles! I can!

Resolution surged through her. Giles deserved the very best of her, and she would not stint in her efforts to get it right for him. *I'll learn how to do it*, she vowed, as she listened to Giles telling her more about Farsdale, the ancestral pile in Yorkshire he would inherit one day.

'Are you sure you want to take it on?' he asked doubtfully. 'It's a bit of a monstrosity, you know!'

She smiled fondly. 'I'll do whatever it takes—I only hope I won't let you down.'

'No!' he answered quickly, taking her hand. She felt warmth go through her. 'You'll never do that! You'll be the most beautiful and wonderful Viscountess we've had in the family!'

Angelos stood, hands curved over the cold metal balustrade of the roof terrace of his London apartment, and gazed out over the river, flowing darkly far below. The darkness of the Thames was shot with gold and scarlet—reflected lights from the buildings either side of its wide expanse. From the penthouse terrace he could see the city stretching far in all directions.

A vast, amorphous conurbation—cities within cities—physically contiguous but socially isolated from each other as if there were stone walls and barbed wire fences between them. The London that he inhabited when he visited the city was the one that had the highest fence around it, the thickest walls, keeping out those who did not qualify for entrance.

The London of the rich.

Many wanted to get in—few succeeded. The failure rate was steep, the odds stacked heavily against them. Passports hard to come by.

Money was one passport—the main one. Those whose endeavours made them sufficient money could gain entry. But sometimes money was not essential, not necessary. Sometimes— Angelos's eyes darkened to match the inky water far below—other attributes would do it.

Especially if you were female.

His hands tightened over the balustrade.

The time-honoured method.

That was what she had used.

He exhaled slowly. He gave an impatient hunching of his shoulders. Well, of course she would! What else did she have?

The cynical twist of his mouth deepened. Only now she wanted more than she had wanted once from him. In the years since then her ambitions had soared—as the dossier he'd ordered showed glaringly.

The Hon. Giles Edward St John Brooke—only son of the fifth Viscount Carriston, principal seat Farsdale, Yorkshire. The Hon. Giles has been a regular escort for the subject at a wide variety of social events over the last year. It is a relationship rumoured in the gossip columns to be potentially one of matrimony, but with the speculative impediment that the Viscount and Viscountess might not approve, preferring a more traditional wife for their heir.

The final phrase echoed in Angelos' head.
...*a more traditional wife...*
His mouth thinned.
Had they had her investigated, being concerned for their son? If so, they would have found only what his own security team had found.

Thea Dauntry, twenty-five years old, fashion model, represented by premier modelling agency Elan. Owns lease of a one-bedroom flat in Covent Garden. British nationality and passport. Born Maragua, Central America, to church-funded aid worker parents who died in an earthquake when she was six. Returned to the U.K. and lived in Church of England boarding school until she was eighteen. Travelled abroad for two years. Started modelling career at twenty-one. Good reputation for reliability. No known drug usage. No other known liaisons other than Giles St John Brooke. Press coverage neglible. No scandals. No record of court orders or police convictions.'

For a second, black fury knifed through him. Then, abruptly, he turned away, stepping back indoors, slicing shut the balcony glass door behind him.

She should be asleep, Thea knew. Yet she was restless, staring sightlessly up into the dark in the bedroom of her Covent Garden apartment. Outside she could hear the noise of the street, subdued now, given the lateness of the hour—well gone midnight. But London never slept. She knew the city. Knew it like a chronic, malign disease. She had lived here all her life. But not in *this* London. This London was a world away, a universe away, from the London she had once known. The London she would never, never know again… never go back to.

And now she would be leaving London completely. She would not miss it—would embrace with gratitude and determination the windswept moors of Yorkshire, the new, wonderful life that was opening out in front of her. Where she would be safe for ever.

But even as she lay there, hearing the subdued noise of the traffic far beyond in the Strand, she felt the shadow feint over her skin. A dark shadow—cruel. Flicking a card down in front of her. A deep, hard voice that had reached out of the past.

But the past was gone—over. It would not come back.

She could not allow it to come back.

Giles phoned in the morning, wanting her to go with him to Farsdale, to be presented with the heirloom engagement ring and meet his parents. But Thea demurred.

'You owe it to them to see them on your own first,' she said. 'I won't cause a breach, Giles, you know that. And I've got a photo shoot this morning anyway.'

'I hope it's for a trousseau,' said Giles warmly. 'To put you in the right frame of mind!'

She laughed, and hung up on him. The troubled, restless unease of the night was gone, vanished in the brightness of the morning. Her heart felt light, as if champagne were bubbling in her veins. The past was gone. Over. Dead. It was *not* coming back. Ever. She would not allow it. And it meant nothing, *nothing*, that a spectre from her past had risen from his damnable earth-filled coffin like that last night!

He can do nothing—nothing! He's powerless! And so what if he's here in London? If he recognised me? I should be glad—triumphant! Because how galling for him to see how I've ended up despite everything he did to me...

She used the defiant, bombastic words deliberately, to rally herself. To give her strength—resolution and determination. The way she always had. The way she'd always had no option but to do…scraping herself off the floor, out of the abyss into which she had been thrust back.

By one man.

The man who, last night, had appeared like a spectre. But the past was gone. She was in the future now. The future she had hungered for all her life. Angelos Petrakos could do nothing do her.

Ever again.

Angelos sat at his vast mahogany desk and drummed his fingers slowly, contemplatively, along its patina. His expression was unreadable, the darkness of his eyes veiled.

Across from him his British PA sat, pencil poised, waiting instructions. He seldom visited London, preferring to run the Petrakos empire from across the Channel, and she was allowing herself the rare opportunity of looking covertly at him. Six foot plus, with broad shoulders and lean hips superbly sheathed in a hand-tailored business suit, strongly planed, ultra-masculine features, and, most compelling of all, dark, veiled, unreadable eyes that sent a kind of shiver through her. What that shiver was, she didn't like to think about too much. Nor about the way his mouth could curve with a harsh, yet sensual edge…

'No other calls while I was in Dublin yesterday? You're certain?'

His PA jumped mentally, summoning back her focus on her work. 'No, sir. Only those I've listed.'

She saw his mouth tighten. Obviously he'd been expecting a call that hadn't come. Fleetingly, his PA felt a pang of sympathy for whoever it was who hadn't phoned when clearly they should have.

Few who failed to do what Angelos Petrakos wanted of them enjoyed his reaction.

Thea walked with brisk purpose along the pavement, heading back to her flat from the local library in the still-light evening of early summer. She was calmer now. Giles was coming back to London tomorrow—she had nothing to fear, nothing to worry about. Relief and gratitude were the only emotions she would allow herself.

As she approached her apartment block, a sleek limo on the other side of the road dimly impinged on her consciousness, but she paid it no notice. This close to the Opera House it would be a chauffeur, waiting for his employer at the theatre. She paused by the block's main entrance, key already out of her bag. There was a second's warning, a footfall behind her. Then a man was standing there, closing her in to the doorway.

'No fuss, please, miss,' said the man.

He pressed the door open, pushed her inside into the entrance lobby. It was done in a second, and for that second Thea was paralysed. Then gut instinct, rising up from the depths, cracked in. She twisted round, knee jerking upwards. There was a grunt from the man, but even as she started to knife back with her elbow, fisting her other hand, ready to stamp down with her heel, there was someone else there—someone who thrust her back powerfully, effortlessly.

Dark, hard eyes looked down at her. She pulled back against the stone wall, eyes distending.

Shock. Panic. Fear.

And far more powerful than any of those— loathing. Black, virulent loathing.

Something moved in his eyes. Then he spoke.

'Still the street rat,' said Angelos Petrakos. He glanced briefly behind him. 'I'll take it from here,' he said dismissively to the bodyguard, who was still catching his breath from the unexpected blow inflicted upon him.

Angelos turned his attention back to the woman

against the wall, her eyes narrowed like a cat's. He could see the pulse hammering in her neck. Immobile she might be, but she had adrenaline kicking through her system.

Well, so did he.

'Upstairs,' he said.

Her eyes narrowed even more. 'Go to hell.' Deliberately, never taking her eyes from him, she reached for her mobile. 'I'm phoning the police,' she said.

'Do it,' he said pleasantly. 'It should make interesting reading in tomorrow's papers. Especially in Yorkshire.'

Her hand hovered, then fell. Her heart was pounding, adrenaline surging round her body in huge, sickening waves. She had to beat it down, get control of herself—of the situation. She straightened herself away from the wall, lengthening her spine, bringing her body into a pose. Regaining the illusion, if nothing else, of composure.

'Why the house call?' she asked. She kept her voice light, incurious.

'I told you to phone me.' His voice was terse. Grating.

She raised delicate eyebrows. 'Whatever for?'

She could see his eyes darken. 'We'll go upstairs

and discuss it.' He saw her hesitate. 'It's in your interest to do so,' he said.

Nothing more. He didn't need it. And he knew she knew that.

Oh, yes, he knew she knew, all right...

Loathing flashed in her eyes, but for all that she turned and walked towards the staircase. He knew why. Even though her flat was on the penultimate floor she would not risk the confinement of the lift. He let her go up first, let his eyes take in the graceful line of her body. She was casually dressed, in a belted sweater dress over leggings and ankle boots, but the dress was cashmere, and the boots the finest soft leather. She wore the outfit with an elegance that might have been natural but which he knew was not. It had been acquired—just as the rest of her image had been acquired. From the sleek fall of her thick blonde hair, caught back in a jewelled grip, to the cultured tones in which she'd told him to go to hell.

But it was all only an illusion—a lie. And now he would be stripping the illusion from her, exposing the lie.

She let him into her flat, setting down her shoulder bag. 'So. Talk.' Her voice came—terse and tense. She was standing hands on hips, chin lifted. Defiance—belligerence—open in her eyes.

For a long moment Angelos simply kept his eyes levelled on her, taking in her new appearance. She hadn't just transformed her image, she'd matured—like a fine vintage wine. Become a woman in the fullness of her beauty. No longer coltish, but slender, graceful. Her beauty luminescent.

He felt an emotion spear within him, but the emotion, like her beauty, was at this moment irrelevant. It was obvious what she was doing. Attacking so she could avoid having to defend herself. He knew why—because she had no defence. Had that street-sharp mind of hers realised that already? He'd shown his hand downstairs, when he'd mentioned Yorkshire—she'd picked it up straight away. Did she realise that the concession she'd made then—not phoning the police—had only proved to him just how absolutely defenceless she was?

Not that that would stop her fighting—defending the indefensible.

Like she'd done before.

His lips pressed tighter. Memory darkening in his eyes.

He let his gaze rest on her a while. Impassive.

Unreadable. Taking his time. Controlling the agenda. Racking up the tension in her. Then, deliberately, he let his glance pass around the well-appointed living room.

'You've done well.' He would allow her that—nothing more.

He could see the flare of her pupils. But, 'Yes,' was all she said.

'And you plan to do better still.' He paused. 'Do you seriously believe,' he demanded, sneering harshness in his voice, 'you can get Giles Brooke to marry you? *You?*'

The flare came again. 'I've already accepted his proposal,' she answered. It was a sweet moment—so very sweet.

She watched his face darken, fury bite in his eyes. The moment became sweeter still.

Then the fury vanished from his eyes. His face became a mask. He strolled over to the sofa, dropping down on it, lengthening his legs, stretching out his arms. Occupying her space. She didn't like it, he could see.

'Thea Dauntry,' he mused. His mockery was open. 'A name fit for the bride of a real, live aristocrat! The Honourable Mrs Giles St John Brooke,' he intoned. 'And then, in the fullness of time, Viscountess Carriston.' He paused—a brief, deadly silence.

Thea felt her stomach fill with acid. She knew what he was going to say…knew it with a sick dread inside her.

His eyes moved over her. Assessingly. Insultingly. Then he spoke. Silkily, lethally.

'So, tell me, what does he think about your little secret? What does he think,' he asked, his voice edged like a blade as cold snaked down her spine and Angelos's malignant gaze pinned her, 'about Kat Jones…?'

The name fell into the space between them. Severing the dam that held the present from the past.

And memory, like a foul, fetid tide, swept through her…

CHAPTER TWO

KAT raced up the escalator at the underground station, not caring if she was hustling the people standing. She *had* to race. She was already twenty minutes late. Half of her told her it was a waste of her time, racing or not. The booker had said as much—the snooty one Kat disliked, who looked at her as if she hadn't washed that morning.

Well, you try keeping lily-white and fragrant in a dump of a bedsit with only a cracked sink in the corner!

Strip washes were all she could manage—mostly in cold water, to avoid the rip-off meter—apart from when she went to the public swimming baths and used the showers there.

One day I'll have a bathroom with a walk-in shower and a bath the size of a hot tub...

There was a long list of things she was going to have 'one day'. And to get even a fraction of the way to getting them she needed this job. *If she could get there in time, before they'd seen all* the girls. *If* they picked her out from the crowd of other hopefuls. *If* that then led to other castings, other jobs, other shoots.

If, if, if...

She took a sharp intake of steadying breath as she thrust through the exit barrier. Yeah, there were a lot of ifs—but so what? She'd got this far, hadn't she? And even this far had been way, way beyond her once.

Everything had been beyond her. She'd had nothing except what the taxpayer had handed out to her at the care home. Who had been responsible for her existence she had hardly any idea. Certainly not who'd fathered her—he probably didn't even know himself. Certainly didn't care. Not enough to check whether the women he slept with ever found themselves pregnant. As for who that lucky woman had been—well, all Kat knew from her records was that she'd been deemed unfit to raise her own child. The social workers had descended when she was five, finding her hungry, crying and with bruises on her thin arms. Her last memory of her home was her mother screaming slurred obscenities at the policewoman and the social worker as they carted her away. Anything else was just a blur.

Just as well, probably.

She'd never settled well, though, in the care home, and had left school the moment she could, resisting attempts to educate her, drifting in and out of casual work, sometimes being sacked for tardiness, sometimes walking out herself because she didn't like to take instructions from people.

But at eighteen Kat had found out something that had changed her life. Changed it completely—for ever. She'd got access to the records of her birth and family. She could still remember the moment when it had happened. She'd been staring down at the paperwork, reading the brief, unexpansive notes written in official language about herself.

Father—unknown. Mother—known to the police as a prostitute, drug addict—no attempt at rehabilitation. Died of drug overdose at twenty-three.

Hatred had seared through her—hatred of the woman whom she could remember only dimly as someone who'd shouted a lot and slapped her, and very often hadn't been there at all, leaving her to pick food out of the fridge, or even the rubbish, and feel sick afterwards. A mother who'd loved her drugs more than she'd loved her daughter.

Yes, hatred was a good emotion to feel about a mother like that.

Then Kat had read the next entry—this time about her mother's parents.

Father—unknown. Mother—a street prostitute, alcoholic. Knocked down by car and killed at twenty. Daughter taken into care.

The chill that had gone through her had iced her bones. For a long time she'd just stared down at the document. Seeing the damnation in it. Each mother damning her daughter. Generation to generation. Then, slowly, very slowly, she'd raised her head. Her eyes had been like burning brands. Her expression fierce, almost savage.

Well, not me! I'm not going that way! I'm getting out—out!

Her resolution was absolute, fusing into every cell in her body. Fuelling, from then on, every moment of her life. She was getting out and heading up. Making something of herself. Getting off the bleak, relentless conveyor belt that was trying to take her down into the pit that had swallowed her mother—her mother's mother.

And two things, it was obvious, could push her down there. Drink and drugs. That was why her mother, and her mother's mother, had become prostitutes, she knew—to fund their addiction. And sex, too, had to be out. Sex got you a father-less baby, raised on benefits, got you trapped into single motherhood. The way her mother had been, and her mother before her…

Sex, drink and drugs—all toxic.

All totally out of her life.

Out too, all the drifting and aimlessness of her existence. From now on, everything had a focus, an end point, a reason. Everything was a step on her journey out of the life she had into the life she wanted. The life she was going to get for herself.

But how was she going to get that life? She was going to work—work her backside off—but doing what? She'd left school with the minimum qualifications, had hated schoolwork anyway, so what could she do?

It was Katya who showed her. Katya, whom she'd met at the hostel for the homeless she'd got a room in, who was Polish, blonde and busty. She palled up with Kat, claiming they had the same name, the same hair colour, the same age—and the same determination to make good. Katya's father was a miner, crippled in an explosion. Her mother had TB. She had eight younger brothers and sisters.

'I look after them,' said Katya simply. She knew exactly how she was going to do so. 'Glamour modelling,' she told Kat openly. 'It makes good money, and at home no one will see those magazines, so I don't care.'

Kat tried to talk her out of it. Her every instinct revolted against going anywhere along that path.

'No. I do it,' said Katya resolutely. She eyed Kat. 'You, with your looks, can model without the glamour,' she said. 'Real modelling.'

Kat had laughed dismissively. 'Thousands of girls want to become models.'

Katya only shrugged. 'So? Some of them make it. Why not you?

Her words echoed in Kat's mind. Resonating like wind chimes, playing seductively in her consciousness.

Why *not* her?

She took to staring at herself in the mirror. She was thin, like a model was. Especially since she didn't spend much on food—not having much to

spend. And she was tall. Long bones. She studied her face. Her eyes were wide. Greyish. Oval
face. Cheekbones high. Straight nose. Bare mouth.
Teeth OK. No lipstick, no eyeshadow. She never
wore make-up. What for, when she avoided sex—
and therefore men—like the plague?

She gave a shrug. Either her face would suit, or
it wouldn't. But she might as well try.

'You need a portfolio,' Katya told her. 'You
know—photos to show how good you can look.
But they cost a lot.'

Kat took a job—two jobs. In the day, six days
a week, she worked in a shoe shop, and in the
evening, seven days a week, she worked as a wait-
ress. She was on time every day. She took all the
instructions she was given without argument, resistance or attitude. She was polite to customers,
even when they were rude to her. She gritted her
teeth, steeled her spine, and did the work—earned
the wages. Saved every penny she could.

It was slow, and it was hard, and it took her six
months to put aside enough. But pound by pound,
doggedly hoarded, she put the money together to
pay for a professional portfolio.

Then she just had to find a photographer. Katya
recommended one. Kat was sceptical, given the

Polish girl's line of work, but Katya went on at her, and eventually Kat said OK. She didn't like Mike, straight off, but Katya was with her, so she didn't walk out. She liked him even less when he wanted her to strip off—just to see her underlying figure, he claimed—nor did she like the fact he didn't like it when she said no. The session took for ever, with Katya redoing her hair and make-up, changing her clothes all the time. She didn't like Mike physically changing her pose, moving her around like a doll. But she knew that was all a model was—a clothes horse. Not a person. She had better get used to it. Train herself to be docile. Even though it went against the grain.

Finally he finished, and when the photos were ready Kat was so stunned she could only stare. The face which all her life hadn't seemed to be anything much, was suddenly, out of nowhere, amazing! Her eyes were huge, her cheekbones like knives, and her mouth—

'I look fantastic,' she said faintly. It was like looking at a stranger—a face that wasn't hers, but was. She gave Katya a hug. *'Thanks!'* she choked.

She didn't see the strange expression fleetingly in the other girl's eyes.

She took the next morning off work and, nerves

shredded like paper, heart thumping, headed for the modelling agency she'd selected as her first try with her new portfolio.

They had, to her exultation, taken her on.

But even after being signed it was a long, slow haul. Assignments were thin on the ground, and competition for them fierce.

Especially the best ones.

Like the one she was racing for now. For a start, the casting was at a seriously flash Park Lane hotel, and the shoot itself was going to be in Monte Carlo—posing on yachts in a marina. She felt a thrill of excitement as she raced out of the tube station. She'd never been abroad in her life, let alone anywhere that fantastically swanky.

As she dashed up to the hotel, heart-rate zapping in her chest, she was intent only on getting to the entrance as fast as possible. She completely ignored the sleek limo pulled up at the kerb, and the frock-coated doorman stepping back from opening the rear door. Nor did she pay the slightest attention to whoever it was getting out. Except that as she raced up to the hotel's revolving door he was in her way.

''Scuse me!' she exclaimed, and made to push past him, to get into the revolving door first.

But the man simply turned his head sharply and stopped, blocking her. Kat glared at him. She took in height, a dark suit, a tanned complexion, strong features which made her pulse give a strange kick, and dark, forbidding eyes clashing with hers.

Her pulse gave that strange kick again. But it was because she was running late, was in a hurry, didn't have time to waste—and this block of a man was in her way. That was why. No other reason.

'Look, are you going to shift or not?' she bit out impatiently, glaring at him belligerently.

Something flashed in the dark eyes. Something that made that kick come again. But it was just because he was still in her way—and because he was looking at her as if she was some inferior being. Her back went up as automatically as the kick that came in her pulse.

'Would you be so very *kind*,' she gritted, in mock-ingratiating accents, 'as to allow me to get into the damn hotel?'

The dark eyes flashed again. But this time it was different. She didn't know how different, or why. But it was. This time it didn't make her pulse kick. It made something arrow in her stomach instead.

Then he stepped back. He said nothing, just indicated with his hand for her to go into the revolving door. It was an offhand gesture—dismissive. She didn't like it. It made her back go up even more. She stepped into the open angle of the doorway, then turned her head.

'Thank you *so* much,' she said, in sweetly acid, exaggerated tones. 'How terribly kind of you!'

Something glinted in his eye, which she didn't like either, and she turned her head sharply and swept inside, pushing the door round, to gain the marbled entrance lobby.

'Posh idiot!' she muttered. Then she pulled her mind away from the incident. She had to find where the casting was.

Fifteen minutes later she was sitting on a spindly gilt chair in a huge hotel function room, looking depressed at the usual horde of fantastic-looking hopefuls. There seemed to be a bit of a lull in the proceedings. The suits at the far end, bunched around a table, must be making their minds up. Kat stared round, feeling strangely edgy—more so than she usually felt at a casting. Maybe it was because she didn't like this room—it made her feel out of place. This was the poshest place she'd ever been in, and all the people who came here were posh. Like the bloke who'd looked down on her for daring to push past him.

Kat's eyebrows drew together. She felt antagonism flick inside her, then pushed the memory out of her mind. No point thinking about it—it had been brief, annoying, and now it was over. Just one of those things. She wondered how long it would take for the suits to decide whether she was one of the lucky chosen.

She wasn't a strong candidate, she knew. Not for a swanky shoot like this. Her looks and style were fine for streetwise stuff, smart and sassy or aggro-cool, but if this was all about yachts then they'd want models that looked the part. Those sleek, classy girls who spoke with plums in their mouths, who were called Christabel and Octavia and knew each other from boarding school. Who were only modelling for a hobby or a lark until they married, or got bored with the hard work it really was.

She went on staring, keeping herself to herself, the way she always did at castings, not caring if other girls thought her standoffish. Then, abruptly, the huddle at the table straightened and a chicly dressed middle-aged woman started reading names out.

Kat's wasn't one of them.

She gave a mental shrug. What had she expected? Disappointment and frustration went with the territory, and you rolled with the punches because there was no alternative. She, like the rest of the girls in the room apart from the chosen nine, who'd hurried forward to the table, started to pick up their stuff and prepared to leave.

Except that, abruptly, another door at the far end of the room opened, close to the table with the suits, and someone walked in.

Kat recognised him instantly, and it set the seal on the casting. It was the man she'd hustled at the entrance to the hotel. By the way the suits had jumped to their feet—even the two women—the guy was clearly a head honcho type. Kat wasn't surprised—it was obvious from the handmade suit to the way he'd looked at her with coldly arrogant eyes, as if she was an inferior being.

Well, if he was the head honcho, then it was just as well she hadn't been picked. She hadn't exactly impressed the guy, had she, back-talking him like that? She hefted her bag, and stood up.

As she did so, she felt something on her. It was the man—he was sweeping a rapid glance over the girls in the room. Maybe he was just checking that the models on the short list, clustered eagerly by the table, were the best there. Well, it wouldn't be her, anyway, not once he'd recognised her. She turned away, moving towards the door.

The voice of the middle-aged woman rang out.

'You—short blonde hair, green shift. Wait.'

Slowly, Kat paused and turned. The woman beckoned to her impatiently.

'Kat Jones, is it?'

Kat nodded, but her eyes went past the woman to the tall figure at her side. The man she'd hustled. Mr Big. His eyes were resting on her. She couldn't read them, not from this distance, but there was something in them that made her feel suddenly very, very weird.

She started to walk towards him.

Angelos Petrakos watched her approach. She appeared wary. He was unsurprised. She'd be ruing her rudeness to him at the hotel entrance. His gaze rested on her critically as she came forward. Too thin for his personal taste, and although her features were stunning, her short, jagged hairstyle was not what he liked in a woman. He liked women chic, elegant, soignée. Not raw off the street like this. With a lip to her that would get her nowhere fast in life.

And yet his eyes narrowed speculatively. There was something about her…

His eyes flicked over her one more time, assessing her. He saw something flash in hers, surprising him. She hadn't liked the way he'd looked her over.

Curious. She was a model—it was her livelihood to be looked over. But she hadn't liked *him* doing it. And that was an anomaly in itself. Women liked him to look them over. They queued up for the privilege. But this *fauve* girl just about had her hackles raised, claws out. Kat was clearly a good name for her…

But her name was irrelevant. So was anything else. The only thing on the agenda was whether she would suit the campaign he wanted—lend an edge to it that more conventional models wouldn't. Well, he'd think about it. He snapped off his surveillance and nodded at the creative director of the advertising agency that had been selected for the campaign.

'Put her on the list,' he instructed. He didn't expand on his choice—that was not the concern of those he paid. He turned to go. 'Have the short-listed girls back here for seven o'clock this evening.'

Then he walked out of the function room.

At five to seven precisely, Kat walked out of the hotel's powder room, where she'd changed into her evening gown, having done her face and hair at home earlier. She was looking good, she knew, and she hung on to the knowledge, knowing her nerves were stretched and she needed all that her reflection could offer her. The thin-strapped *eau de nil* silk gown bought in a sale fell sheer down her slender body, its pale colouring suiting her own paleness. Strappy, high-heeled sandals lifted her hips and gave an assertive boost to her stride.

But beneath the surface her emotions were conflicted. Predominant was nervousness—but running alongside that was another emotion. One that she didn't want to feel.

She knew who he was now—she'd had it spelt out to her by the suits after he'd walked out of the room that afternoon. Angelos Petrakos. He wasn't the guy who owned the yacht company—he was the guy who owned the company that owned the yacht company.

Yeah, well, she thought bitingly to herself as

she strode into the hotel lobby, she wasn't going to tiptoe around him, however much she wanted the job. If he wanted to hire her—fine. But no way was she kow-towing to him! No way!

She still didn't know why he'd put her on the short list. She was a completely different type from the sleek, posh others. Well, she didn't care about that, either. Either she'd be picked or she wouldn't. That was it, really. Nothing to do with her—just what Mr Big wanted.

She felt an odd sensation jitter through her. It was different from the impulse she'd had to slug the guy for looking at her like meat. Yet it still had something to do with him looking at her. She frowned as she walked along. It wasn't a feeling she'd had before. It felt alien. Unnerving. She found, too, that she was replaying the encounter at the hotel door in her head—and then the bit where she'd been summoned to the table. The odd jittery sensation went through her again.

She didn't like it. It made her feel—vulnerable.

And vulnerable was something she never, never wanted to feel.

Quickening her pace, she headed up the broad sweep of stairs up to the function suite. Inside, she saw that the other nine girls were already there—

and so was Mr Big, talking to the most important suit. Deliberately not looking at him, Kat took her place beside the group, standing quietly to one side.

Angelos looked up. Immediately his eyes went to girl he'd added to the short list. His gaze stilled.

She was looking stunning. With part of his mind he tried to analyse why—and failed. Every girl here looked outstandingly beautiful, yet there was something about the edgy blonde that made her stand out even from them—that made him want to look at her…

Was that quality, whatever it was, enough to make him break the brief he'd given his creative team? That the models for this campaign should have the glossy, upmarket look that went with the new line of luxury yachts Petrakos Marine was launching? He turned to his creative director, taking a seat at the table and tilting his chair back slightly.

'Have the girls walk,' he instructed.

Deliberately he studied the other girls as they paraded up and down as if they were on a runway. Then, equally deliberately, he let his eyes go to the edgy blonde.

She doesn't like it, surmised Angelos. She doesn't like parading up and down on command. Doesn't like taking orders. Showing herself off. He could see her resentment in every stiffened line of her body as she stalked up and down.

'That's enough.'

The girls stopped, came back to the table. The creative director leant forward to say something to Angelos, but he held out a hand to silence him. His gaze remained on the girls clustering around. He worked his gaze along them, his face expressionless.

Then he simply said, 'You, you, you,' nodding at each he'd chosen in turn.

One was blonde, with long hair down to her waist—clearly her particular asset—the second was an aristocratic brunette, and the third was Eurasian and any man's private fantasy. They would all be ideal for the campaign.

Having made the required decision, he left everything else to his staff. But as he got to his feet his eyes went to the girl at the end of the row. She looked even more apart than before. The other rejected girls were peeling off into a group, some shrugging, some looking unconcerned, while the favoured three were taken off by two of his staff to get more details of the forthcoming shoot.

For a long moment the girl in the *eau de nil* silk just stood there, very still. Her face was quite expressionless. Then she turned away, walking back to the door.

There wasn't any sign of resentment now. Only deliberate indifference.

Except that it wasn't indifference. He could see exactly what it was—defiance. Not by the slightest slump of her shoulders letting any trace of having been rejected show. He watched her a moment, ignoring whatever it was his creative director was saying to him.

Then he went after her.

He caught her up just in the upper foyer, as she was heading for the stairs down and out of the hotel. He took her arm.

She stopped dead and jerked around. Her eyes flashed.

'Don't handle the merchandise, sunshine!' she said, and made to tug away. It had no effect on his grip.

Angelos looked down at her upturned face. There was antagonism bristling in her eyes, but more than that. Something behind the antagonism.

'There may be room for one more model. I'm prepared to consider it,' he said.

Something flashed in her eyes, then disappeared.

He let go of her arm. 'I'll discuss it with you in my suite.'

Her eyes flashed again, but not with the emotion that had just been in them.

'Get stuffed,' she said, and wheeled round. He caught her again.

'You mistake me,' he said, and his voice was icy. 'This concerns merely whether you are, or are not, suitable for this campaign. Nothing else.' He walked towards the bank of lifts, not bothering to see if she was following. She would be, he knew.

She stepped into the lift beside him, standing as far away from him as possible, staring straight ahead, her shoulders rigid. Wary as a cat, but with a hunger, he knew perfectly well, for what he had in his power to offer her. As the elevator lifted away he caught the faintest tang of perfume—something citrusy. Sharp. It suited her, he realised.

Beside him, Kat stood, every nerve end bristling. It had been a rollercoaster all afternoon—from realising she wasn't going to be short-listed to the exultation that she had been, and then, just now, the bitter knowledge that she still hadn't made it, despite her best shot and her evening gown.

Only to have hope flare all over again—

She felt pincers snip away inside her stomach. And now it was not just because of the job she wanted so much. It was because of the man she was standing beside. Something about him was setting her nerves jangling.

It's because he's an arrogant s.o.b—that's why! Mr High-and-Mighty, Filthy-Rich-Big! Looking at me like I'm nothing more than meat.

And it was in his power to give her a job she really, really wanted.

No other reason. Absolutely no other reason.

As she walked after him into the suite she stopped dead, gazing round, mouth dropping open. So this was how the rich lived! The place was like some kind of apartment, with rooms opening off a lounge that had a balcony on one side and a dining table in a huge alcove. Two huge sofas faced each other across an acre of coffee table.

'Sit down and wait.'

The voice was indifferent, assuming obedience. She did as she was told, still looking around her,

and then her eyes went to him without her volition, watching as he extracted some papers from a
briefcase, setting them down upon the dining table
and standing to look through them. He started to
make phone calls in a foreign language. It didn't
sound like anything she'd heard before, so maybe
it was Greek—the guy was Greek, the model
who'd told her about him downstairs had said.
Greek—and loaded.

And not just with money.

Kat found herself looking at him. Staring at
him.

He might be an arrogant s.o.b, but she knew
exactly how he was getting away with it. With
looks like his—all that height and toughness and
hard, planed features and dark, measuring eyes,
plus that magnetic Mediterranean appeal with his
olive skin tone and sable hair and that indefinable
aura of being 'foreign'—he must have women sla-
vering for him!

Oh, not her. No chance. Because she didn't
slaver over *any* man, and never would. But she
could still feel her nerves jangling, and she didn't
like it. Didn't like it one bit. Every impulse told
her to jump to her feet and run, but she had to sit
there, like a good little girl, because this man—

however much her made her hackles rise—could give her the job she craved.

Her eyes flashed momentarily. *But I'm still not kow-towing to him! He can take the job and stuff it before I do that!*

She set her jaw, forcing her eyes away from where he stood, looking as if he owned the place. Which he might very well do, she realized. He was stuck giving orders in Greek, or whatever it was, down the phone. Her eyes went back to looking over this room where the rich folk hung out, taking it all in—the décor, the furniture, the deep carpets, the vast bouquet of flowers on the sideboard. All the trappings of luxury that a man as rich as Mr Big took for granted every moment of his gilded life.

A world away from her own life.

Well, she would never get to this level—she knew that—but then she didn't want to. Didn't need to. All she needed was something a lot better than she had—a clean, nicely furnished flat, not the squalid, mouldering bedsit she was holed up in now, and enough money coming in for her not to be cold in winter and watching every penny every minute of the day. Something that was hers and hers alone—a decent life.

And one day she'd have it. One day—

Her focus snapped back to the present. The phone calls had stopped, and he slid the phone away in his inside jacket pocket, coming across to sit down opposite her in an armchair. He'd helped himself to a drink from somewhere, but wasn't offering her one, she noticed. Just as well. She wouldn't have touched it.

He hooked one leg over his knee and relaxed back into his seat, holding his glass in his hand. His eyes rested on her.

Kat made her face expressionless. She was learning how to do that.

'So…' said Angelos Petrakos. His voice was deep, but with hardly a trace of accent, she realised, only the clipped, curt tones of a posh Englishman—a million miles away from the London voice *she* spoke with. 'Shall I hire you, or not?'

Kat's expression didn't change. Was she supposed to answer, or just sit there like a dummy? She chose to answer. It was probably the wrong thing to do, but sitting voiceless was more than she could make herself do.

'No point asking me,' said Kat. 'I'm just the meat.' Her voice was deadpan.

'Meat?' The word fell into the space, ready frozen.

She tightened her mouth. 'Clothes horse. Dress rack. Dummy. AKA body. AKA meat.'

His eyes seemed to narrow minutely. 'You have a problem with that?'

She shrugged. 'It's what modelling's all about,' she answered.

'But you object?' The voice was sardonic.

'Not if I get paid. And if I don't get any hassle,' she added pointedly.

For a moment he did not answer. Then the dark eyes narrowed again. For a moment Kat felt she was skating on thin ice—very thin ice—that might suddenly crack, disastrously, and send her plunging down into dark, drowning water…

Then it was gone.

'And if…*hassle*…were part of the deal?'

For answer, Kat held up a single finger, her face expressionless.

Angelos's eyes flickered to it, then back to the girl's face. Why was he doing this? He had no intention of sleeping with her. His assessment was purely professional. But something made him say, his tone suddenly dulcet, 'You might find it enjoyable—'

'And you,' Kat retorted sweetly, 'might find the attempt painful.'

For a second, the barest portion of one, she felt the ice give an ominous crack. As if he might actually find her answer amusing. Then the hard features hardened even more, and he simply levelled upon her a glance that crushed her like an insect.

Oh, God, thought Kat. *My big mouth.*

But Angelos Petrakos was reaching for his mobile phone. It was answered instantly. He didn't look at her. 'Add Kat Jones to the shoot,' he said.

She stared, eyes widening. Then elation soared through her.

A moment later it dissipated. Those sharp dark eyes were back on her again.

'Provisionally,' said Angelos Petrakos.

She looked at him warily. 'What's that mean?' she asked. She sounded blunter than she'd meant to, but her nerves were jangling for a hundred reasons which had a lot more to do with the hard-featured face of the man with the power to hire her than the job he was dangling in front of her.

'It means,' he answered, 'that I want to check whether you can behave appropriately. Fit in. I don't tolerate,' he said cuttingly, 'attitude.'

Kat bit her lip. She could feel herself doing it. Forcing herself to do it.

'Exactly,' said Angelos Petrakos, a mordant expression in his night-dark eyes. Then, abruptly, he got to his feet. 'If you have any engagements for this evening, cancel them.'

She stared. Wariness radiated instantly from her again, like a beacon switch thrown to high. He saw it—just as he'd seen her forcing herself to bite her lip.

'I'm taking you to dinner,' he enunciated. 'There will be a considerable amount of socialising in Monte Carlo. The other girls will find it easy. *You* need practice,' he told her coolly. 'If, that is, you are to go at all.'

CHAPTER THREE

KAT had got the message, loud and clear. She was on trial. And, whilst one part of her wanted to tell him what he could do with his 'provisional' offer, the other side of her brain managed to hold down that predictable but destructive reaction.

The trouble was, she realized, as she stiffly and self-consciously followed Angelos Petrakos down in the lift to the hotel restaurant with determined docility, that trying to behave 'appropriately'—she mentally gave the patronising term a vicious nip—for going to Monte Carlo was being impeded by the very man who was judging her behaviour. Because as she jerkily took her place opposite him in the ultra-swanky restaurant—all dim lights and designer seating and damask linen—the tension she felt was not just because of her surroundings—or the fact this job depended on her behaviour, but predominantly and overwhelmingly because spending any time at all in the man's company was stringing her nerves out like wires.

She didn't want to be here. She didn't want a bevy of waiters hovering around, flicking out napkins, proffering water, bread, menus, so that she didn't know what to do or what to take or what to say. And she didn't want to open a huge leather-bound menu and stare blankly at the entire thing, written in French, not understanding a word of it. It made her feel like a fool, and she resented it. *And* the man who was putting her through it. Above all she didn't want to be anywhere near *him*.

Because—well, just because. That was good enough, wasn't it? she told herself aggrievedly. She didn't have to say she didn't like the way his strong features made her want to look at them, even though they damn well shouldn't have, or the way his dark, glinting eyes seemed to flick over her like a blade and do things to her that they shouldn't, or the way his handmade suit eased across his broad shoulders and the silk slash of a tie accentuated his aura of Mr Big, so that everyone flunkeyed around him and he didn't even notice it.

'Chosen what you want yet?' His voice was cool as he addressed her.

She pressed her lips together. 'I don't know. I can't read it. It's in French.'

She was being truculent, she knew, but couldn't stop herself. The place was getting to her. *He* was getting to her.

'You'll find,' replied Angelos Petrakos, his sarcasm silky, 'that French is the *de rigueur* language in Monte Carlo.'

Kat gave a shrug, doggedly resistant to his put-down. 'Well, I'll be stuffed then, won't I?' She shut the menu. 'I'll have a green salad, no dressing. That OK in a place like this?'

She was sounding belligerent, and she really, really didn't mean to. It was stupid to be like this—just stupid! But she couldn't help herself. She felt wired all along her nerve endings, a tightness in her chest.

He was frowning. 'That's all?'

'Yeah. Model—diet—you know.'

She was being daft, not just flippant. This was free food. She should eat a week's worth and starve till the weekend! But right now she didn't think she was going to be able to swallow easily she was so strung out.

A second later her nerves twanged like a bass guitar. His eyes were resting on her. Just—resting.

But it was all they had to do. Suddenly her dress seemed skimpy, her breasts too noticeable beneath the slinky fabric, her shoulders and arms far too exposed. She felt—naked.

Not in the way that photographers and stylists made her feel—although she hated that, no mistake—but what was happening now was…different.

Worse. Much, much worse.

Because when photographers and stylists made her feel like meat it didn't make her feel like this.

As if she was suddenly burning hot and freezing cold at the same time. As if she wanted to jump to her feet and bolt, and yet was glued immobile. As if her breathing had stopped completely, and yet her heart-rate was racing as if she'd just injected adrenaline straight into it…

And then suddenly the gaze was gone, and there was, instead, a faint frown line between his brows, as though yet again something had annoyed him.

Then the waiter was hovering, ready to take orders. She repeated her request for salad, her voice sounding tight and breathless. When he'd gone, Angelos Petrakos turned his attention back to her.

'You'd look better with more flesh on you,' he said. He sounded critical, and it galled her. But then, everything about him galled her. Or did something like that to her...

'Tell that to the camera,' she riposted. 'It puts weight on if you just breathe.'

'So you live on air?'

'Just about. You get used to it.'

The frown between his eyes snapped deeper. 'With the aid of drugs?' he shot at her.

'No,' she retorted instantly. She said nothing else. It was a subject she never discussed. Never.

'Good,' he said brusquely. 'I don't tolerate drug-users, for any reason.'

She didn't answer. There wasn't anything to say. She knew drugs were prevalent in the modelling business, both for recreation and weight control, but since she didn't socialise she saw very little of it.

Then a guy with a little metal cup beetled up, with a minion in tow bearing a bottle as if it was some kind of baby. Kat stared, nonplussed, at the ritual that then proceeded.

'What was that all about?' she heard herself

asking, as the flunkey and his minion beetled off again, having eventually filled two glasses.

Angelos found himself explaining the role of the sommelier. While he did so he wondered, for the dozenth time, what the hell he was doing right now. Bringing this ill-mannered, back-talking, street-sharp girl here to dinner. Oh, he knew what he'd told her—but that wasn't the reason and he knew it. He couldn't care less if she was gauche and unsophisticated on the shoot, provided she took instructions and shot well. No, he had different reasons for extending his time with her—reasons he didn't want to focus on right now, simply continue with.

She was totally not the type of female he was ever interested in—too thin and too raw, with an unlovely London accent exacerbating her sharp tongue. A universe away from the sophisticated and soignée women he chose for company.

So why was he wasting his valuable time on this mouthy, angular, bony female who'd brought her back-street behaviour with her from whatever sink estate she'd been dragged up on?

The question probed at him, finding no answer. None but whatever it had been about her that had made him subject her to his scrutiny from the

moment she'd pushed past him in the hotel doorway to now, having her sit here opposite him,
clearly completely out of her social depth and
radiating resentment, hostility and, most obvious
of all, having to force herself not to jump to her
feet and march out of the restaurant and high-tail
it back to wherever she hailed from.

Was that it? he found himself wondering. Was
that why he was wasting his time on her? Because
she didn't want him to? Because she so obviously
didn't want his attention?

Something he'd never known in any female. Oh,
the women he associated with were sufficiently
sophisticated not to let their assiduous desire to
please him be conspicuous, but it was there all the
same—all the time. He took it for granted that it
would be, even if it was just his wealth alone that
drew them. And if the kind of women he selected
for his relaxation were of that mind, how much
more so all the other females who crossed his
path in more workaday, humbler roles? A girl in
this model's circumstances should be desperate
to court his approval, impress him with her suit-
ability for the assignment.

For a fleeting moment he examined the possibil-
ity that the girl was deliberately trying to make

herself noticeable by being as belligerent and hostile as she was. Then he dismissed it. No, her body language—bristling and protective—was genuine. So was her resistance and suspicion. His eyes darkened momentarily. She'd repulsed very clearly, very crudely, his deliberately voiced and entirely theoretical proposition. Had she meant it? It had seemed entirely spontaneous, entirely genuine. But... He found his thoughts turning over. Would that resistance last if he let her think that his selection of her as an extra model for the yacht shoot was contingent on her supplying sexual favours?

Was she *really*, despite her sharp tongue and bristling body language, that virtuous?

His thoughts idled. Perhaps he should put it to the test...

Out of nowhere, like an image illuminated by dark light, he saw her in his mind's eye, her elongated, coltish body lying on a bed, her small breasts bared, her head tilted back, pale hair jagged on the pillow, eyes blinded by a moment of sexual whiteout—

He thrust the mental vision aside forcefully. The last thing he was interested in was taking her to bed! Forcibly, he focussed his mind on the present circumstances—wondering what on earth had possessed him to waste dinner in her company. She was as far from his type as it was possible to be, and with every minute that passed she confirmed it. Her ignorance was total. She had clearly never dined in a restaurant like this before, and clearly never made conversation over a dinner table before. Her brusqueness was comprehensive, at every question or comment he made, whether from nerves or belligerence.

On top of the ludicrous green salad she'd insisted on, she was ignoring the wine poured for her. Instead, she reached for her water glass and drank it down. Angelos watched her.

'You won't try the wine?'

She set down her empty glass and shook her head. 'I don't drink,' she said. 'Empty calories.'

It was all the reason she would give. Besides, she found talking hard. Her jitters were getting worse. She didn't like the way she was getting more aware of the man opposite her. He seemed to be crowding her consciousness, making her look at him, and she didn't want to. For a searing second she could feel an urgent impulse to grab the glass of wine and knock it back. A second later she crushed the impulse. No. No alcohol.

Ever. End of story. Instead she took a steadying breath, swallowing air to calm her.

He made no reply to her terse rebuff, only lifting his own wineglass, taking a slow mouthful of wine, swirling the ruby liquid in the large glass, his eyes still resting on her. She shifted position, wishing she could just get up and go. It was like being under a microscope. She hated it. Then, like a release, he set down his glass and turned his attention to his food. Kat felt her stomach cramp with hunger as he forked the rich, fragrant dish of seafood.

He started a new topic. 'Tell me—have you been to Monaco before?'

'No. I've never been anywhere.' Why had she said that? He didn't need to know she'd never been anywhere.

His fork stilled. 'You've never been abroad?'

'No.' She collected herself, clamming up.

The dark eyes rested on her. She hadn't a clue what was going on in them. Didn't care, anyway. Why should she? If he wanted to make stupid conversation with her, she didn't have to make it back. Couldn't anyway. She knew that. Knew she knew nothing. And didn't care either.

I just care about getting this job.

He was speaking again, taking another considered mouthful of wine. 'That's rare, these days, even for the British,' he observed.

Kat shrugged.

'You never went abroad on holiday as a child, with your parents?'

'No.' She'd never been on holiday, period. As for her parents—a junkie, prostitute mother and an unknown, could-be-anyone father didn't really cut the mustard when it came to taking their darling daughter off on foreign jaunts...

Anger spiked through her suddenly. Anger at what this man was digging out of her. She turned it towards him to get rid of it—the quickest way she could. 'Look, what *is* this?' she demanded belligerently. 'What's it to you whether I've ever been abroad or not? I haven't—OK? Is that some kind of crime in your book?'

The hard features hardened abruptly. 'I told you I don't tolerate attitude,' he bit out at her. 'Do you *really* have no idea how to conduct yourself? Because, if so, perhaps I should reconsider my decision.'

He watched with satisfaction as emotion jabbed in her eyes, then subsided.

He nodded. 'Yes, that's better.'

He resumed eating. Was the girl really worth the trouble, after all? Yet even as he questioned himself his eyes were going back to her. Taking in those high cheekbones, the luminous skin, the extraordinary eyes focused once more on picking at her salad, the jagged blonde hair edging the sculpted line of her chin. Raw, rough, resistant—yet she drew the eye. And not just his.

He could see it in the other diners. Females were glancing at her, and not just because she was dining with him. He could see she was making them feel as if they themselves were overdressed, fussy, with too much make-up, too elaborate a hairstyle. As for the men—they were looking at her because she was completely, supremely, not paying them attention.

And that quality—that ability to draw eyes—was all that mattered about her. Not her rudeness, her insolence, her thinness, her ignorance.

She'd started to eat finally, forking the green salad mechanically. How the hell she lived on such a diet he couldn't imagine. But presumably she did it because she had to—competition amongst models was ferocious, and she was right: the camera *did* add weight. Did she really not do drugs? he mused. His eyes glanced at her arms, but they were unblemished—though that was hardly proof positive. She'd seemed adamant, however, and anyway drug usage was an instant termination of contract clause for models.

As she ate, she made no attempt to talk to him—didn't even look at him, or anywhere else. Illogically a flicker of annoyance went through him. The last thing he wanted was the girl getting any ideas, yet at the same time being so totally blanked by her made his mouth tighten. He reached for his wine again, taking another contemplative mouthful as his eyes rested on her. For a moment he found himself wondering whether, by some remote chance, the girl had any hidden depths to her. It was extremely unlikely, of course. Nevertheless, having insisted on her presence, he should interrogate her for the purpose he'd stated.

'So,' he began, 'what do you know of Monte Carlo, even if you've never been there?'

Her eyes snapped up. 'It's full of rich people,' she said.

'Anything else?' The voice was silky again, as if he was holding on to his patience.

Kat shrugged one shoulder, not replying.

'Are you in the slightest bit interested in knowing anything more?' The silk was wrapping a blade now. She could hear it, and her resentment mounted. Why should he care whether she knew anything about the place?

'What for?' she retorted.

There was a flicker across the dark eyes, and for a moment she felt she'd pushed back too much.

'To demonstrate to me, perhaps—' now the blade was cutting through the silk '—that despite being ignorant, which is probably no fault of your own, you possess sufficient native intelligence to want to know more about the world than your educationally limited and culturally deprived background has afforded you?'

Heat flushed through her, then cold.

Angelos took a mouthful of wine, then set down his glass with a click on the table.

'To be ignorant is one thing—to want to remain so is another,' he said.

Kat felt her blood sting. *Patronising bastard! Smug, conceited, patronising bastard!*

God, she wanted out of here! Out of this place where she felt like some kind of dirt under the sole of a pair of handmade shoes! Where Mr Big sat lording it over her, sneering at her and patronising her, and above all holding in his hands the power to give her this job or snatch it from her when she'd come so close to getting it!

And, worst of all, making her feel not just like some lowlife but that horrible hot and cold at the same time—as if there was ice in her veins and a hot stone in her stomach, and as if her nerves had itching powder in them. She'd never felt that before and never, never wanted to feel it again...

She wanted to get to her feet and go—just *go*! But she gritted her teeth, swallowing it down. She could do this—she could! It would be worth it. It would get her the job and that was all she cared about! He wanted her to know about Monaco? So she'd find out—if that was what he wanted!

'I'll find a guidebook about the place,' she said.

Her voice was tight, and she was obviously speaking under duress, but the recalcitrance had gone—or at least was being suppressed.

'Do that,' he said, and went on with his meal.

He kept her under surveillance as he ate. Could he really be thinking of considering her in any light other than a professional one? Considering silencing her provocative, insolent mouth in a way that he found was suddenly vivid in his imagination...?

He was still undecided. It irritated him that he

should be so. He made decisions fast in his life—the demands of running a multinational corporation necessitated swift, accurate, unhesitating decisions. So why was this girl making him think twice? Why was he even thinking about her at all? Considering her for his bed?

Round the question went in his mind again, and again it found no answer.

Nor had it still when, the last leaf of rocket disposed of, Kat Jones looked up and said bluntly to him, 'Can I go home now?'

Angelos pushed aside his own empty plate and reached for his wineglass again. His eyebrows rose questioningly.

'Can I go home now?' Kat said again. She was as tense as a board, he could see. Maybe his reprimand for her rudeness had unnerved her—brought home to her how…unwise…such behaviour was.

And maybe it was as well if she went now. Rushing her into bed on an impulse he still couldn't fathom himself, would also be…unwise. Although it was also tempting.

Did he really want to let her go? His eyes went to her again, assessingly. Deliberately he let himself take in every aspect of what she had on offer…

Across the table Kat froze, unable to breathe.

A hole, a gaping slash, had opened up inside her. And she was falling—falling right down into it.

Oh, God, no—no!

She could only stare helplessly, appalled, as Angelos Petrakos looked her over.

It was like it had been before, as if she couldn't breathe, and yet her heart was pounding, making her feel that impossible mix of shivering cold and burning hot. Her veins felt as if they were melting…as if he was melting them…because of the way those dark, steel-hard eyes were working over her, reaching a place that no one had ever reached before…

She tried to fight it. Tried with a desperation she hadn't known she would ever need.

No! You are not going to let yourself…let yourself…

She clawed back sanity. She didn't do sex. She fielded it, ignored it. It didn't exist. Just didn't exist. She didn't *let* it exist.

But now, in a single glance, she knew how totally, completely wrong she had been…

He snapped off the gaze. And like a rag doll, limp and bereft of breath, Kat could only sit there—powerless, appalled.

Oh, God, what had just happened? Why? Why this man?

She had to go. Right now. The imperative of it overwhelmed her. The need for flight. Flight from something she could not cope with—just could not cope with.

'I really have to go.' She heard herself say the words. Heard them fall like stones. Tight, abrupt. Would he think she was lipping him again? She didn't care? Couldn't afford to care—just had to go, get out.

While she still could…

She dumped her napkin on the tabletop, jerking to her feet. 'I'm sorry. I've got an early start tomorrow.' She sounded disjointed, but she couldn't help it. Couldn't help anything right now.

He'd got to his feet as well. It registered dimly with her, and for a moment she panicked, thinking she wouldn't be able to get away. Then she realised he was simply standing because she had. She forced herself to look at him. His face was shuttered again, his expression veiled. But she didn't dare look at his eyes. Didn't dare meet them…not again.

'Thank you for dinner,' she got out, still in that disjointed manner. 'But I really do have to go.'

She stared around, trying to remember where the restaurant entrance was. A waiter came gliding over. Angelos Petrakos said something to him, and the man murmured acquiescently and glided off again.

Angelos turned back to Kat. 'A taxi will take you home,' he said.

'I can't afford—' she began automatically, but he simply raised a hand.

'The fare is taken care of,' he replied.

'Oh. Thanks. Um—' She fell silent. She was desperate to ask— *So, are you going to hire me? Am I going on the shoot?*

But she didn't dare. Didn't dare do anything except pick up her evening purse from the tabletop and clutch it for dear life.

'Goodnight, Kat,' said Angelos Petrakos to her. His eyes were still veiled, still unreadable. Her veins were still in meltdown. She had to get out— now. Right now.

Angelos watched her go, nearly bumping into other tables in her haste. Almost, he went after her. Instead, he resumed his seat. Another waiter glided up, removing the empty plates, bringing him his entrée. He started to eat, quite mechanically. His mind only on one thing.

Kat Jones. And what to do about her.

He made his decision.

Kat sat, collapsed, in the back of the taxi. She should have luxuriated in the ease of the journey, but she was still in shock. More than shock. Worse than shock. She was like one of those native peoples who suddenly got exposed to germs they had never had. Keeling over.

Oh, God, where did it come from? And why? Why him? The guy's an arrogant bastard—rich and almighty, Mr Big and Powerful. And I don't want, I don't want, I don't want to feel like this. I don't!

But she did. That was the awful part of it. And it was the weirdest, shakiest feeling. She kept wanting to replay it in her head, make his face come up in front of her, see him there as if he was real. Over and over again.

No! What are you thinking of? Just stop it—stop it!

But it was like an electric switch that couldn't be turned off again. It was on when she went to sleep, on when she woke up. On when she went to work.

Even her anxiety as to whether or not she had

or hadn't managed to get on the Monaco shoot couldn't turn it off. Yet she knew, with her head, that the shoot was the *only* thing she must think about—worry about.

The moment she could she phoned the agency on her mobile, desperate for news, crossing every finger and toe as she asked the snooty cow Anita if they'd heard anything yet from the Petrakos Marine campaign managers. It took another two covert calls from the shoe shop's storeroom before Anita's condescension turned to ill-concealed chagrin—and sent elation soaring through Kat.

The ad agency had been in touch—she was on the shoot. And the fee that Anita grudgingly told her was…well, fantastic money! Loads more than she'd ever made before!

She punched the air, and for the rest of the morning floated off the ground.

This was it—her big break! It had to be! Her first real money! Serious stuff! And with this shoot in the bag she'd be up for more of the same—and better. She was on the way—she was really, really on the way! The pit she'd crawled out of was getting further and further away, and she was reaching for the sun…

Nothing could drag her down now. Nothing…

As for Mr Big, and the insane way she'd reacted to him—well, even if he showed up during the shoot she'd just stay clear of him, that was all. She'd have to. She damn well wasn't about to—

But her thoughts stopped right there. Anything else was mad. That was all she had to remember. Mad.

Keep focussed—the job is all that matters. Nothing else.

It was what she had to hang on to. She'd lived without sex in her life, and she'd go on doing so. And certainly not with someone like Angelos Petrakos.

He'd use you and lose you.

Her spine steeled. No, it didn't matter that she'd reacted the insane way she had last night. She'd got the job, and that was all that mattered.

That day she had to work through her lunch hour to make up for time she'd taken off to go to yesterday afternoon's casting, but she didn't care. Nothing could crush her elation—not now! She worked late, too, so she could make time to call in at the agency first thing tomorrow to sign the paperwork for the contract. She was still floating, all the way back to her bedsit, but as she walked from the bus stop her feet abruptly sank to the ground—along with her elation. Mike was hovering at the kerb, his motorbike engine idling. *Oh, hell*, was her first thought. She could really do without the guy right now! Why didn't he just give in and accept she wasn't interested? Instead of pestering her like this and hanging around, turning up when he wasn't wanted—would never be wanted. She started to walk along the narrow pavement. He drew level with her on the bike.

'Mike,' she began, 'look, I really don't have time for this—'

He steered his bike across her path, blocking it. He took his helmet off. Kat stopped dead and gave a heavy, exasperated sigh, glaring at him.

There was something different about him, she registered. It was his eyes. They were glittery.

'No time for me, baby? That it?' he said.

'Mike—' she tried again, but he cut right across her.

'But you've got time to hang out with your loaded rich guy, haven't you? I saw you last night in that hotel, schmoozing him, coming on to him!'

She stared. 'How did you—?'

He laughed harshly. 'I followed you! I follow you everywhere! You showed up at the hotel in the afternoon, and then again in the evening. I walked in and saw you in the restaurant with him. So you come across for rich guys, do you, baby?'

Anger spat through her. 'I was there for a casting, that's all!'

He laughed again—derisively. 'Yeah, casting couch. You put out for him and he gives you the job! Well, don't worry, baby. That suits me fine.'

'Get lost!' she snarled at him. She made to get past him, around the back of the bike. His hand shot out and closed over her arm. It was like a vice. She yanked to free herself, and failed. 'Let me go!'

For answer, he just hauled her forward, almost up against him. Fear suddenly spiked through her. The road was deserted, the streetlight broken, and it wasn't a good part of town in the first place.

'Uh-uh, babe. I'm fed up with giving you slack, OK? Time for you to put out for *me*.'

'In your dreams!' she spat at him, again trying to yank herself free. Anger overriding her fear now.

He gave another laugh. His eyes glittered more intensely. She realised, with a jolt, that he was high.

'Uh-uh. In my photos. Oh, come on, baby— what d'ya think I want? Sure, I want to screw you first, but then it's for the *punters*, see? Now, you may think they only like big girls like Katya, but trust me, babe, they like skinnies like you, too. I'll make you look really hot! You'll make good money, don't worry!'

He grinned at her. Kat's face contorted. She lashed out with her foot, impacting his shin, tugging back on her arm again. But Mike was strong. Frighteningly strong. He yanked her closer.

'Wanna fight me, babe?' Something glinted in his free hand, and with sick horror Kat realised it was a blade. He whipped it to her cheek. 'Just how hot will your modelling career be when you've been razored? So let's do this nicely, huh?' Then, suddenly, his tone changed. ''Course, you could always keep me happy another way. Now you're screwing Mr Rich you can afford to be generous. You pay me what he's paying you, and we'll call it quits, OK?'

She could feel the edge of the blade, flat on. All he had to do was twist his wrist…

Terror and sickness dissolved her. 'O…OK,' she managed to get out.

He smiled. 'That's good.' He slid the flat of the blade down her cheek. 'Shame to mark you.

You're worth more unmarked. So, how much are you going to bring me?'

'A…a hundred,' she said shakily.

He laughed nastily. 'Get real, babe. Just bring me the lot, OK? Cash, jewellery—whatever he pays you in. Don't hold out on me, now. I'll be watching you. Like I always do. Wherever you go, baby—wherever you go.'

As quickly as it had appeared the blade was gone and he was thrusting her back. Pulling his helmet on and climbing on his bike. She stood, shaking, on the pavement. He turned to smile at her. His eyes were like pits.

'Like I say, shame to mark beautiful girls. But…' He sighed. 'Sometimes they just don't learn. Like your friend Katya. She didn't want to put out for the punters. Now she couldn't sell herself to a blind man!' He laughed, a sound as sick as the words he'd just said, gunned the engine, and roared off down the road.

Somehow Kat made it back to her bedsit, shaking like a leaf. With fumbling hands she found her mobile. When Katya answered she sounded distraught.

'I'm sorry,' she kept saying. 'I'm sorry. He was already threatening me when I got you in for your portfolio shots. He's been after you since then. Kat, do what he wants! Whatever he wants! Photos, money, men—just do it! Don't say no to him, Kat! Don't say no!' Kat could hear, through her own terror, Katya's.

'Oh, God,' she whispered. 'What did he do?'

There was a silence. Then, 'He cut my breasts. He cut them and cut them. All over.'

CHAPTER FOUR

KAT was calm—very calm. It was her only option. Otherwise she would break down into hysteria. She knew what she had to do. The police would be useless. Unless they gave her round-the-clock protection, Mike would always find her. Would always be trailing her. Stalking her. Threatening her. She would have to buy him off the way he wanted—buy herself time until, with the money from the Monte Carlo shoot, she could hire her own protection and work to get Mike caught for attacking Katya and threatening herself. Once she'd got a signed contract surely she could raise cash on the expectation? Enough to keep Mike at bay for now?

She headed for the agency.

Anita was at her desk. She was looking pleased with herself. 'Oh, there you are, sweetie. I've been trying to reach you. About the Monte Carlo shoot.' She smiled sweetly. 'They don't want you after all.'

Kat heard the words. But they didn't make sense. 'What do you mean?' Her voice was hollow.

'I mean they don't want you any more.' Anita's lip curled. 'Well, they did specify "classy", and that's hardly you, is it?'

'But I've got to have that job,' Kat heard herself say. From very, very far away.

Anita laughed—a tinkling sound. 'Too bad,' she purred.

Too bad—the words echoed in Kat's head as her feet took her out of the agency, took her along the busy London pavement. She could feel fear start to crawl over her skin, memory bringing back the sick glitter in Mike's eyes, the sicker glint of his knife-blade—the same blade that had cut Katya's breasts…

I've got to have that job. It's the only way to get Mike off me. I've got to get it back.

As she walked, thoughts—hectic, panicked— crowded into her brain. Dismay washed through her. Cold, like icy water. Angelos Petrakos had turned her down after all—and she knew why. Like a stone in her guts, she knew exactly why.

It's my own fault! He warned me, but I still couldn't keep my mouth shut. That's why he's pulled me from the shoot! That's why! But I don't

*understand. Why did they say I was on it yester-
day and then pull me? How come one minute I'm
on, the next I'm off! How could he change his
mind like that? I don't get it—I just don't get it!*

Confusion, dismay, and sick, gutting fear
writhed within her. In her mind she saw Mike's
knife glint in the light, heard Katya's terrified
warning. Desperation scythed through her. She
could do a runner—head out of London. But that
would be to run from everything she'd achieved
so far, to start all over again. And where? London
was where the big modelling contracts were. Like
the one she'd just lost.

*I've got to get it back! I've got to try, at least!
If I go to him—beg, crawl—maybe he'll change
his mind back again. I'll be as meek and docile
as he wants! Whatever it takes!*

It was all she could do, and she knew it. Rage,
fury, anger—all were useless now. Useless! Fear
churned in her stomach. She had to batten it down.
Keep it under control. Tight, tight control.

She went to the hotel first. It was the only place
she knew to go. She walked up to the swanky receptionist and asked for him. The woman looked
at her coolly.

'Mr Petrakos is not in his suite,' she told her. 'Try his office.'

'But I don't know—'

Kat stopped, and walked away. She found a library. Looked up 'Petrakos Marine', and the name of the boat company. It was all she could remember. She tracked down a London office for Petrakos International U.K. Phoned the number. Got passed around. Then, finally, 'Mr Petrakos is in Dublin today. He'll be back tonight and in the office tomorrow.'

Relief washed through her. For all she'd known Angelos Petrakos could be back in Greece now— or on the other side of the world. But he was coming back to London. He hadn't checked out of his suite. He'd be there tonight.

And so would she.

To prostrate herself before the almighty Angelos Petrakos and beg him to hire her after all.

Angelos rolled his shoulders and massaged the nape of his neck. His jacket was draped over the back of a chair, his tie likewise. It had been a long day. But tomorrow he'd set an easier pace—with a highly enjoyable evening to look forward to.

Courtesy of Kat Jones.

He'd made the right decision, he knew. He wasn't about to question it any further. It would be, he knew, *electric*. Kat Jones was so utterly different from his usual choice of woman. True, that meant that his affair with her would be highly restricted—but, however brief, it would be enjoyable. He looked forward to seeing her wary antagonism towards him change to something very different...

For a moment he considered getting in touch with her now, but decided against it. He had things to go through from his Dublin meeting that he wanted to be shot of first. He strolled to the sideboard, slipping his cufflinks and dropping them on to its surface, following suit with his watch, turning up his shirt-cuffs. He picked up the first report and lowered himself down on the sofa to read it. A minute later the doorbell sounded. That would be the suite butler, bringing his coffee. Absently he pressed the console to open the door for him, his eyes swiftly perusing the words in front of him.

He heard the door open, but paid no attention. The man knew his business, and knew not to disturb hotel guests. Then something—instinct, or the faint catch of body scent—made him whip his head round.

Kat Jones had walked into his suite.

She stood very still. Her heart was pounding. Adrenaline surging in her body. Crackling through her like overloaded static.

Mike was outside in the street—he'd been dogging her footsteps all day, trailing her on his motorbike. Keeping the sick fear churning inside her. Now he was waiting outside the hotel. Not close enough to draw the attention of the doorman. Close enough to make sure she saw him. Saw him lift a finger to his own cheek and draw it down, slowly, deliberately. Smiling at her.

She got the message. Right in her terror centre.

Now, as she walked into Angelos Petrakos's suite, she felt as if a garrotte were strangling her.

I've got to get that job back.

Angelos Petrakos got to his feet. She saw him, but it was as if he was underwater, or behind glass, very far away.

'Kat.'

She heard her name. Heard the deep, accented voice. Heard it and felt it do things to her. Things that didn't matter. Not now, when all that mattered was why she was here.

'I was not expecting you,' he said. His tone was even, but his expression was veiled.

'I—I wanted to see you.' How she got the words out she didn't know. They came out as a low husk. It was all she could manage through her stricken throat.

A hollow was opening up in her stomach. Her eyes had gone to him immediately as he'd stood up, taking in his jacketless state, seeing the white shirt taut across his lean chest, the strong column of his throat framed by his open collar, the mus-cled sinews of his bare forearms and his turned-back cuffs. Then her eyes had shifted upwards to the strong-featured face, the sable hair, the narrowed, night-dark eyes. Something shifted in them as her eyes went to him, but their expression was still veiled.

'Indeed?' It was all he said. His face was a mask, but behind it she was having the same impact on him now as she'd had that first evening—those ex-traordinary luminous eyes, the high cheekbones, the mobile mouth, and that incredible wand-slim body. Even though, he registered, there was far less of it on show this time. Her outfit was not an evening dress. Instead, he registered, it was some kind of day-dress, grey, and buttoned all the way down to her knees, with long sleeves and white cuffs.

It should have looked demure, as it was designed to. Instead…

He snapped his mind away. What was Kat Jones doing here? Even as he framed the question he supplied the answer. One that told him when a woman showed up at this time of night there was only one reason why…

Emotion knifed through him, but he put it on hold. Waiting. Watching.

The sound of the door chime made her jump, but Angelos simply pressed the console again. This time it was, indeed, the suite butler. He batted not an impassive eyelid to see a woman present, merely fetched another cup and saucer from the sideboard and added it to the tray. Kat was grateful for his presence—it bought her precious time in which to try and compose herself, dissipate the appalling tension stringing her out. She set her clutch bag down on the sideboard, flexing her stiff, clenched fingers. She tried to steady her breathing, loosen the garrotte around her throat, drain out the hideous sick feeling permeating her.

There was silence while the butler did his business, then departed.

'Coffee, Kat?' said Angelos.

His voice was smooth. There was something in it she did not recognise. She shook her head, watching while Angelos Petrakos poured his own black coffee.

'Perhaps you'd prefer something stronger? A liqueur, perhaps?' He indicated a tray on the sideboard, with a variety of bottles on it. 'I may,' he said ruminatively, 'take a cognac myself.'

Again she shook her head jerkily, watching, heart slugging heavily, while he set down his coffee cup beside the tray and poured himself a measure of brandy, swirling it contemplatively in the rounded glass as his eyes rested on her.

They were completely shuttered. She couldn't tell anything about how he was thinking. What he was thinking. She stared at him, eyes distended. *Do it! Say it! You've got to!*

'Mr Petrakos…' Her voice was breathy. Husky. 'I—I wanted…wanted…to—to apologise to you…'

She had taken him by surprise. He had not been expecting this. Apologies and Kat Jones were not things he would associate together. His eyes narrowed infinitesimally. The emotion he had first experienced on seeing her in his suite like this intensified.

She stumbled on, words halting, her voice still with that husky breathiness. 'Over dinner the other night, I was…I was…out of order. It was because…because I'm not used to places like this.' She gestured jerkily with her hand around the suite. 'Flash places. Fancy restaurants. It made me…nervous. Maybe I came across as…rude…'

He made no reply, just went on resting his eyes on her. She had no option but to go on.

'So I wanted to…to ask you…if…if I promise I won't behave like that again—because I won't—I really won't—if…if…you would give me another chance and…and reconsider your decision about the Monte Carlo shoot. My agency told me—' She swallowed, biting back the emotion that cracked in her throat. 'Told me that you'd changed your mind about me after all. I want to change it back again,' she husked. 'Persuade you to take me back on. I really, really want to do that! And if you did I would be so, so grateful…'

Her voice trailed off. Her mouth was dry. She could feel every high-pressure pump of her heart, every racked muscle of her body. She'd done it—

done what she'd come to do. Crawled and begged and pleaded. Abased herself before him. Because downstairs—waiting in the shadows, waiting for her to come out of the hotel—was a madman with a razor, waiting for a chance to use it on her...

'So very grateful,' she breathed.

Angelos stilled. Every muscle in his body stilled. The brandy swirling slowly in his glass stilled. Then slowly, very slowly, he started to set it in motion again.

She was gazing at him—eyes wide, distended. Lips parted. Her breasts rising and falling as she breathed. He took it all in, eyes resting on her. There was no expression in them. But inside emotion knifed, its stroke slicing through him. Then he spoke.

'How grateful, Kat?'

The smoothness in his voice was gone. Instead there was something that, just for a moment, seemed to slither over her skin.

'How grateful, Kat?' he said again.

The words fell into the air. She stared at him. Words forming in her mind that she could never say. *There's a psycho down on the street who wants to slash my face open if I don't pay him what I'll earn from that shoot—that's how grate-*

ful I'd be! But that wasn't what she could say. All she could say was, her voice still husky with tension, '*Very* grateful.'

It galled her. Every fibre in her being rebelled at what she was doing—begging, pleading with this man, humbling herself to the man who could save her with a single word, or send her back out on to the street to where Mike waited for her with his razor.

He did it to Katya—he'll do it to me!

Fear gutted her again—fear laced with a stabbing urge just to yell at this man she was crawling to, yell at him to give her the job back, just give her the job back because she needed it—needed it desperately…

He had set down his brandy glass on the sideboard. His eyes were still resting on her. Veiled, unreadable. She could feel her heart slugging in her chest as she waited for the answer that would save her…or doom her. Desperate hope fused with churning terror…

Angelos watched her. Watched her through the mask of control that had iced over him. But underneath the nameless emotion knifing through him had revealed itself.

Cold, black anger.

Memory bit through him. Her sitting on that very sofa, making that crude, forceful riposte she'd made when he'd baited her about sexual favours in the line of her work. For all its crudity, it had been that that had told him what he needed to know to make the decision about her that he had, knowing that—however hungry she was to obtain modelling work on the marina shoot—she possessed enough raw integrity to reject using her body to advance her career.

And now—

So much for her parade of virtue! Now she was ready to offer anything he wanted to get what she wanted...to show her 'gratitude'...

His anger intensified.

He'd wanted her. Made a decision to follow through on what he felt about her that had, against all expectation, piqued his interest. And now he was being balked of it. Balked at this very moment now, at this late hour of the night, in his private suite, when she was standing there, her raw physicality impacting on every nerve ending, that demure, white-collared dress of hers signalling an erotic appeal that was making him compellingly aware of the body beneath, with its small, high breasts, slight hips and long, slender legs. Even the unstyled hair, pushed behind her ears, only framed her face more—that extraordinary face…

He wanted her. And now he could not have her. Because he never, ever indulged a woman who wanted him to advance her career for her… To do so would be to compromise his principles, to give in to a temptation to indulge himself that he would not allow himself. He had too much self-respect, instilled into him all his life, to do as Kat Jones now wanted him to. Anger knifed again. It needed a target.

He walked towards her, stopping dead in front of her. Then lifted his hand. Cupping her cheek with his palm.

Kat froze. Every muscle in her body froze. What was happening? What was he doing? Why—? She could only stare at him, eyes huge, distended. He was too close—far too close. How had he got so close? Why…?

And then, as if her sensory system were working in slow-motion, she felt the tips of his fingers feathering along the line of her hair. A thousand nerve endings shimmered and she gave a tiny strangled gasp in her throat. His thumb moved leisurely, exploringly over the tender lobe of her

JULIA JAMES

101

ear. Faintness drummed at her. Heat flushed up the column of her throat, beating like a wing. Sensation was thrumming through her like fire licking along her flesh…

Nothing else existed. Nothing except what he was doing to her. Touching her, stroking her. He was looking down at her, holding her, enclosing her. Forming her whole world so that nothing else existed at all. Nothing other than this could ever exist…

He was blanking out everything—all consciousness, all memory, all awareness other than this moment, *now*. Weakness flushed through her, leaving nothing behind. No memory of why she was here, no memory of what had brought her here…

Only this exquisite, unbearable sensation.

He was saying something. She could hardly hear it, but then it penetrated—penetrated through the mesh of sensation he was engendering.

'How grateful, Kat? This grateful?' There was darkness in the eyes looking down at her, looking right into her. 'Or this?'

His hand grazed down the line of her jaw. He eased the tips of his fingers across her throat, settled on the button at her collar. He slipped it loose, then moved with the lightest, most lethal touch to the next button. He slipped that too, feathering at the skin beneath.

His other hand slid around the nape of her neck and drew her to him.

She could not stop him. Could no more stop him than she could have stopped the ocean. Her body slackened against him. She had no strength, no will, no conscious thought.

His mouth closed over hers.

It was a deep, sensual kiss. He did not intend it to be otherwise. It was, after all, all he would have of her...

Kat was drowning. Drowning in the sea of sensation that had closed over her head, her mind—every particle of her being. The drowning went on and on and on, dissolving her, so that there was nothing left of her, only the incredible sensation exploding in her. From away, words formed...

So this is a kiss...

She had never been kissed before. Never allowed a man near her. Never.

And now...

Now she was being taken—her mouth by his—her senses overwhelmed, and she had never known that it was possible to feel like this, to feel such sensation…such incredible, intoxicating arousal, such melting of the flesh…

There was no more reality—only this. This endless, intoxicating sensuality.

And then his mouth was lifting from hers. She could only gaze mindlessly, dazed, into his eyes—those night-dark eyes. They flickered over her and she felt heat deep inside her. His hand still held her nape, and without its grip she would have swayed, collapsed, for there were no bones left in her body, no thoughts in her mind, no consciousness of anything other than this—this obliterating, consuming *now* that had taken her into a world she had never known existed.

He was looking down at her. His eyes were still veiled, unreadable.

Then he spoke.

'That was good, Kat,' he said. 'Very—*grateful*…' His voice was a drawl, like talons over hardest stone.

He dropped his hands from her and stepped back. She swayed, but he made no move to steady her. There was incomprehension in her face—more than incomprehension—and something about it fed his anger. She was trying to speak, he could see, but there was nothing he wanted to hear. Nothing he wanted from her—except what he could not have. What she had made impossible.

His eyes steeled. Time to finish this.

'But, despite your spectacular body, Kat, and your eagerness to bestow it upon me in gratitude for advancing your career—' his gaze washed over her like acid '—I must disappoint your ambitions.'

She stared. She had been drowning—drowning deep, deep in an ocean of sensuality that she had never known existed, never dreamt existed. And now suddenly she had been beached, was gasping for air, cold sucking at her.

Oh, God, what had happened? What had happened? What did I let him do to me? How could I have—? How could I?

Her thoughts were rags, torn and shredded. What was he saying to her? She had crawled to him—abased herself to ask, *beg* for the job she *had* to have… But what had he done? What had she let him do? What was he saying…?

She fought for comprehension.

It came—like a killing blow.

'I have no interest, Kat—' his voice razored '—in bedding whores. And what else is a "grateful" woman offering her body than a whore?'

Time stopped. Rushed up from the past, searing across her brain. Words were spearing into her—bald, typed notes, impinging themselves on her retinas.

...known to work as a prostitute...

The pit beneath her feet opened. Yawned like the mouth of hell to swallow her up, take her to that place of damnation which had swallowed up her mother, and her mother's mother.

But it would never, *never* swallow her!

She could feel the rage. Feel the fury. Boiling up in her. Boiling over.

'Don't you *dare* call me that!'

He laughed. Harsh. Contemptuous. 'You stand there, at this hour of the night, offering yourself to me to show your *gratitude* if I give you back that modelling job, and yet you deny that you are whoring yourself to me?'

Her face contorted, rage ripping from her. 'It was *you*! *You* moved in on me!'

'To teach you a lesson! That *no* woman makes use of me!' His eyes skewered her, pinioning her on lasered points. 'Get out of here. Now.'

Emotion boiled in her—rage, blind rage, at *him*. Saying that to her! Doing that to her! And then, like a punch in her guts, the other reality returned.

The sick, terrifying reality of why she had come here…

Oh, God! Mike was still downstairs—waiting for her.

Waiting with his razor, his mad, drug-fuelled sickness.

Terror exploded in her. She flew at the man standing there, calling her such vile things, ripping from her the one thing that she was desperate for—*desperate*! Her face contorted, her fists pummelling impotently at the steel wall of his chest as she pounded at him with all her strength, fury and venom spitting from her.

'You offered me that job!' she hurled at him, ripping words from her twisting mouth. 'The agency *told* me the offer was there! They told me the fee and the schedule and everything! And then you yanked it back again! What do you think you're playing at, you arrogant *jerk*?'

He thrust her back as if she were nothing more than a rag doll. She stumbled backwards, impacting the sideboard, clutching at its surface to get her balance, lungs pounding, fury burning through her. Her hand closed over something— she didn't know what, didn't register it, registered only that in the intensity of her anger she was panting, breathless, her head a maelstrom of emotion.

'You absolute *bastard*,' she said in a shaking, vehement voice. 'I *crawled* to you! And that's what I got for it! To be called a *whore*!'

He cut her vicious diatribe with a single utterance, eyes black. 'Get out, Kat—or I'll get Security to do it.'

His voice was like ice. Annihilating her. Throwing her out—with nothing. Nothing to keep her safe from that sick psycho downstairs. Nothing to keep his razor from her face...

Her hands spasmed, terror convulsing her fingers, and as they did she felt the shape of what her right hand had closed over.

It was a watch.

Like some kind of nightmare replay, she heard Mike's voice in her head. *Just bring me the lot, OK? Cash, jewellery—whatever...*

Slowly, without any conscious will, she tightened her grip on what she held. Time and reality slid away. Her mind wasn't moving. Nothing was moving. Her chest felt as if it was going to explode, as if she could not draw breath.

As if from the bottom of a deep, deep well she watched Angelos Petrakos stride to the door and yank it open. And as he did so, she turned. She saw—her eyes not registering, her mind suddenly totally blank—saw her hand move, saw her other hand reach for her clutch bag further along the sideboard, saw herself slip the wristwatch inside—the wristwatch of a man so rich it *must* be valuable—closing the flap of the bag to conceal it.

'*Out—now.*'

Angelos Petrakos's voice knifed into her.

She turned back. She had stopped existing. Someone else had taken over. Someone who was walking towards the door blindly, unseeingly. It wasn't her any more—not her clutching her bag to her chest, where it burned against her like a flaming brand, walking past Angelis Petrakos, who had turned her boneless with his touch and then called her a whore. It wasn't her—it wasn't her. It couldn't be her. It couldn't be…

It couldn't be her walking across the silent, deserted corridor to step into the empty lift and plummet down, down, down, the weight of the bag clutched against her like a stone—it couldn't be her…

Inside her head, a voice was yelling. *Take it*

back! Say something—anything! But take it back.
Or leave it here—in the lift!

But she couldn't do that. The person who had
taken the watch was telling her she couldn't do
that. She had to take it to Mike, waiting out in the
street, the razor in his jacket pocket.

The elevator doors sliced open. The hotel lobby
yawned ahead of her. She walked out, shoes clip-
ping on the marbled surface of the polished floor.
It was late. The lobby was all but empty. The large,
revolving doors of the exit were motionless. She
went towards them, heart pounding inside her, skin
blanched, muscles screaming with tension. She
didn't look to left or right. Didn't see the concierge
put down his phone, nod at someone at his side.
Didn't see the security guard walking towards her
until, as she lifted her hand to push at the revolving
door, he stepped up to her. Stopping her dead.

'Excuse me, miss. Would you step this way?'
he said.

The police station was quiet at that time of night.
Kat waited silently beside the officers who had
come to the hotel to arrest her, summoned by the
hotel's security department. Angelos Petrakos, it
seemed, had been swift to notice the absence of his

watch—swifter still to phone down and have her intercepted before she could get out of the hotel. Now, she'd been impassively informed, he was on his way to the police station to make a formal identification—both of her and his watch…his custom-made platinum watch with its diamond face and handmade Swiss mechanism.

She knew she would be charged with its theft. She would let herself be charged.

As she'd got into the police car outside the hotel she'd seen, across the road, Mike on his motor-bike. And she had known, with sick terror, that if she walked out of the police station with nothing to give him she would be at his mercy. For a fleeting instant she wondered whether to tell the police officers about him. But they wouldn't believe her—they would think she was saying it to divert them from her theft—and, anyway, what could they do?

At least in prison she would be safe—safe from Mike…

Hysteria beaded within her, but she crushed it down. Crushed down everything—all thought, all emotion. Everything was over. Everything was finished. Her life would be destroyed—just as her mother's had been, her grandmother's before her. There was no way out now—not from what she'd done.

Now she was answering the officer's questions—name, date of birth, address—numbly, docilely. Because what else was there to do? Nothing could save her now. Only a miracle. And they didn't happen. They *never* happened.

A policeman was walking into the station—yellow reflective coat on, boots and a helmet. A traffic cop. He walked up to the desk. Face sombre.

'What's up?' asked the sergeant.

'Nasty business—just happened,' said the traffic cop, shaking his head. 'Motorbike speeding—skidded and smashed head-first into a wall. Just round the corner from here. Rider dead on impact. The ambulance is there now, taking the body away.'

'Any ID?' asked the sergeant.

The traffic cop dropped a driving licence on to the desk. Kat's eyes went to the photo. The world stopped moving. It was Mike.

For a timeless instant she could only stare. Not daring to believe.

Not daring to believe in miracles.

Then, as if an electric charge had jolted through her, she knew what she must do. What she had to do to save herself—to save herself from the pit of destruction that was opening beneath her feet.

There *was* a way to save herself—if she took it—if she snatched at it—snatched at the lie that glowed in front of her like a lifeline. She could use it to haul herself out of the pit that was swallowing her up even as she sat there, waiting to be charged with theft, to have her life ruined, destroyed—over. Her brain was working feverishly, desperately. She had to do this—she *had* to! It was her only chance.

She had to become the person she had been in that nightmare moment in the suite, when her hand had closed over the watch. Ruthless, desperate.

She took a breath—jagged in her throat—opened her mouth, touched the sleeve of the policeman taking down her details. Interrupting him.

She made her voice match the lie—the lie that might save her skin. Save herself from prison. From having her life destroyed.

'Officer,' she husked, 'I need to speak to you... discreetly...'

Angelos's mobile rang. He answered it immediately.

'Yes?' he barked. His limo was paused at traffic

lights, the chauffeur revving the engine expectantly. The blue light of the police station was visible a short way beyond.

There was a pause. Then, 'She's saying *what*?'

The policemen, his voice impassive, repeated what he had just said. 'Miss Jones is denying absolutely that she is in possession of stolen property. She is saying,' he went on, his tone studiedly deadpan, 'that you gave her the watch as a present, sir.' He paused slightly, choosing his words with care. 'A *personal* present. Following her visit to your suite this evening.'

He let the words sink in, then resumed. 'In the circumstances, therefore, Mr Petrakos, we would advise you that we will not be charging Miss Jones. It would, after all, be your word against hers. Especially considering that as I understand it she has a witness in a hotel employee who saw she was there with your consent, and that you were offering her hospitality. Moreover, Miss Jones says she appreciates you may have changed your mind about making her such a generous gift, and has returned it. We have therefore discharged Miss Jones, and your watch is now in safe custody, awaiting collection.'

Angelos's grip tightened. The beds of his fingernails were white. White the lines around his mouth.

Then, 'Thank you, officer,' he said. 'I will be there shortly.'

There was nothing in his voice. Nothing at all.

As the limo glided smoothly forward, approaching the police station, he could see a tall, slim figure pause at the entrance, start to walk down the steps. The limo pulled into the car park.

He was out of the car before she had set foot on the pavement. Blocking her way. He seized her arm. It was as if an iron claw had closed around it. She stared blindly up into Angelos Petrakos's murderous face.

For one endless moment he just stared down at her.

Then slowly, each word dragged from him, he spoke.

'You try and sell me your body, and when I don't buy, you dare—you *dare*—to steal from me! And then you slime your way out of it by lying about me! No one—*no one*—steals from me and lies their way out of it by slandering me, accusing me of paying for sex!' His eyes sliced her, sharper than a razorblade. 'Enjoy this moment—it's all you'll have. You're finished.'

Then he thrust her away from him and she fell—down, down, down, into the pit he'd opened beneath her feet.

CHAPTER FIVE

THE destruction had been systematic and ruthless. The power of Angelos Petrakos had seen to that. Her contract with the agency had been cancelled, and no other London modelling agency would take her on—unwilling to risk the wrath of so rich and powerful a man. He'd had her evicted from her bedsit, sacked from her day job. Everything Kat had achieved by sweat, hard work, and dogged willpower was gone.

He'd left her with nothing.

Nothing but her will.

And the memory of what he had done to her.

And now, five long years later, the memory burned with a livid, coruscating flame in her head, giving her the strength she needed now to defy him. Because defiance was all she would *ever* feel towards him! She had refused to stay beaten—refused to go back down into the pit. Though he'd ripped her life to shreds she'd climbed back up, hand over hand, out of the pit.

And when she'd emerged she had no longer been Kat Jones. She would never be Kat Jones again…

Whatever Angelos Petrakos threatened her with.

Her eyes were steely, meeting his head-on, unflinching.

'Get out of my flat,' she said. Her voice was level, even if below the surface she was fracturing into tiny pieces.

'You haven't answered my question.' Angelos's voice was implacable. 'What does your *fiancé*—' he made the word mocking '—think about Kat Jones?'

Her silence was tangible. That and the whitening along her cheekbones revealed everything to him he needed to know. His eyes glittered darkly.

'You haven't told him.'

It was not a question.

For an endless moment his eyes simply hooked hers in their talons. She tried to tear them away, but could not—could only stand there while he eviscerated her with his eyes. With his words.

'You deceitful, manipulative little liar,' he said softly. 'You were going to marry him, weren't you? Knowing he was getting a mirage, a fake? *Weren't you?*'

The fury was naked in his voice, icing through

her. She couldn't move—couldn't speak. Dread filled her.

And something more than dread. Something worse.

She could feel the adrenaline leap in her body and tried to crush it down. Not because it fed her anger—she didn't care about her anger, she welcomed it, needed it—but because it fed a quite different emotion. One that was deadly to her. Lethal. One she could not, *could not*, allow herself to feel.

She straightened her spine. 'Get out,' she said again. She could feel the pulse in her throat throb. It was loathing—that was all. Loathing that it was signalling. Nothing else. She wouldn't allow it to be anything else.

He didn't move. Stayed right where he was, occupying her sofa. Invading her space. Her life. Forcing her nightmare past into the present she had made for herself—into the future she so desperately wanted with Giles.

Then he spoke. 'You have a choice.' His words cut like a knife through flesh. Her flesh. 'I will not allow you to inflict your deceit upon that hapless fool you've got in your toils. Either you tell him about Kat—or I will.'

'No!' The word broke from her—instinctive, urgent. Kat Jones was gone—gone for ever! She would never allow her back—never!

He smiled. The smile of a predator who had seen his prey trip and fall.

'Oh, yes, Kat. You'll tell him. Or I will do it for you. Do you really think—' his dark eyes rested on her with implacable condemnation '—I won't?'

No. She didn't think that. She knew *exactly* what Angelos Petrakos would do. He always did what he promised he would do—she knew that... Oh, how she knew that!

Dread and rage surged in her. But there was something else as well—something that forced its way to the fore, cutting through both those turgidly swirling emotions.

She could never tell Giles what Angelos was demanding. Never! Because she knew that for Giles it would make no difference. Hollowness emptied her. Giles would abide by the code of his class, and nothing on earth would make him abandon it! Whatever she told him, he would say that he had asked her to marry him and no power could make him retract that! He would stand by her even knowing what she had told him, despite all that...

And she couldn't do it to him! She couldn't!

'Which is it to be, Kat?' Angelos's voice pierced her. 'You or I to tell that deluded English lordling of yours that you're a thief, a liar and a whore?'

'I *never* offered myself to you! Never! And you got your watch back!' she gritted. 'You got it back!'

A harsh rasp escaped him. Black rage showed in his face. 'You claimed it as payment. Painted me as a man who pays for sex. You stole from me, Kat, and you lied about me. And you thought you could get away with it!'

Her hands were clenched. Heart hammering in her chest.

'You *destroyed* me! You took everything—everything from me! You took my livelihood, my career, even the lousy flea-pit I lived in! You took everything! You told me you'd finish me, and you *did*!'

Long lashes dipped down over his eyes. His voice was edged like a sharpened blade. 'But you didn't stay finished, did you, Kat? You've crawled back. And you're more ambitious than ever! But I won't permit you to make a fool of that poor, hapless sap of yours! He deserves the truth about you!'

'No.' Her rejection was absolute. She could not do it to Giles—could not condemn him to marry a woman like Kat, knowing her to *be* Kat, knowing what she was, where she came from, what she had done…

And even though she would—*must!*—refuse to marry him, she could not bear to see the expression in his eyes when he realised how she had deceived him.

'No,' she said again, her voice tight as wire, garroting her.

Heaviness crushed her. Truth, insistent and brutal, forced itself upon her. Like blows on her head. Reality slammed into her and hatred burned in her eyes for Angelos Petrakos. Hatred not just for him, but for what he was forcing on her—making her accept, bitterly, reluctantly. She could not deceive poor Giles, could not use him the way she had—for what else could it ever have been to let him marry a woman not knowing what she once had been?

The garrote tightened around her neck, choking her.

Angelos could see her expression, see her horror, her fury. Something shifted in his eyes again, curved the thinned line of his mouth.

'Or you can have one more choice, Kat,' he said. His eyes glittered darkly with black fire. 'I'll let you keep the fiction you've created about yourself, but if you haven't the guts to tell him that you're really Kat Jones then you can release him from your toils another way.' The malevolent glitter of his eyes speared her. 'Tell him you've changed your mind about marrying him.'

'Why would he believe me?' She forced the words from her narrowed throat.

He smiled, his mouth mocking, obsidian eyes alight with an unholy light. 'Why? Because, Kat, the love of your life has just walked back into it...'

She could only stare. 'You're insane,' she breathed.

'An effective fiction—and it will serve the purpose I intend. To convince him, Kat, and to remove yourself from his vicinity after you've told him that—alas—you can no longer marry him, you'll come to me. Spend the night at my hotel.'

'I will never do that—*never*!' Her face and her voice were stark.

'You prefer the alternative? For him to know who you really are? Not that sanitised, white-washed fairy tale you've concocted about yourself?' He got to his feet, walked to the door, and as he twisted the handle he turned. 'Be grateful that I make you this offer. This way the Honourable Giles need never know about Kat Jones. And once he's free from you, you can keep your shiny new image, your lucrative new career.' He paused, letting his gaze rest on her one more time, his eyes like granite.

'The choice is yours, Kat. And you have twenty-four hours in which to make it. If you're not at my hotel tomorrow evening at nine I shall know what you've chosen—and act accordingly.'

Then he was gone.

Alone, Thea stood quite, quite still. Then slowly, very slowly, she wrapped her arms about her body. Very, very tight. In front of her the pit stood gaping. And she had no choice, no choice at all, but to step into it.

She could feel herself falling, feel the air being sucked from her lungs as she plummeted down into the pit that Angelos Petrakos had opened beneath her feet. Her guts were hollowed out, muscles in her legs seizing up. She was in some kind of shock, she knew. In disbelieving, aghast denial—desperately trying not to believe what had just happened and yet knowing with every particle of her being that it was true.

Angelos Petrakos had destroyed her—again.

Her arms clutched around her body. Her eyes were bleached with stricken emotion.

She might not love Giles—what *was* love? She'd never known it in her life—but she cared for him, and she would never, never hurt him by telling him how she had deceived him. She had no choice—she must let him go. Let go her dream—the one that she had yearned for, striven for, and so very, very nearly achieved.

Anguish at what she was losing twisted in her. Then, in its wake, came anger—blind and hot, seeking a target. She heard Angelos Petrakos's caustic voice—'*You didn't stay finished, did you?*'

No, she hadn't! Despite everything—everything he'd done to her—she'd got out of the pit he'd thrown her into! Made a new life for herself!

Her eyes hardened and she loosed her protective cradling of her body, her hands instead forming fists, tensed at her sides. She lifted her chin, unseeing as her gaze burned with the bright, intense light of pure will, pure determination. Resolution seared through her.

I've survived Angelos Petrakos before, and I will do it again!

For a long, timeless moment she went on standing there, hands clenched, face like stone, as emotion burned in her. Then, as if with a slow exhalation of breath, she let it go. With a strange, preternatural calmness in her breast she went to put away her library books and resume her interrupted evening. Tomorrow, everything would change, but this last night she would spend as she had planned—a quiet supper, a Mozart CD, and a good book to read.

Enough to gather her strength for the ordeal ahead. The ordeal she would survive. The ordeal she *must* survive.

But for all her resolution, telling Giles when he returned to London the next morning that she could not marry him was a slow agony. The pain in his eyes crucified her. But she had to inflict it. There was no other way. She could not—could not—tell him the truth. Yet to stop him wanting to honour his offer of marriage, as she knew he would, she had to hurt him with another lie—and such a monstrous one. Of all the people in the world, it was the one she loathed with all her being whom she now had to lie about! The lie mocked her with whips—and so did Giles' response.

'You're still in love with him, aren't you?' said Giles.

Thea couldn't speak, could only nod. 'I'm so sorry,' she whispered. 'So terribly, terribly sorry. I lied to you in that restaurant, denying I knew him, because I desperately wanted it all to be over between him and me. But...he came to me last night and—' She couldn't go on. The vileness of the lie she had to tell was too great for that.

'I'm just so sorry,' she whispered again.

He patted her hand. A jerky movement. His face was not showing much. He never let emotions show. Not deep ones. But she knew he felt them. He was a good, kind man. A decent, honourable man. A man she would have striven with every fibre of her being to be a good wife to.

And now—

It was over. The dream she had dreamt was over before it began. Despair racked her. And anger and shame, and a regret for what could never now be so powerful that it crushed her.

'I can only wish you every happiness,' said Giles.

She gazed at him with stricken eyes. 'I'm so sorry,' she said again. 'And I hope and pray with all my heart that you find a woman more worthy of you.'

He would never know just what she meant by that. But *she* would know, and the knowledge incised deep into her. Only the certain knowledge of her own misery could assuage the pain she was inflicting.

Sadly, guiltily, she kissed his cheek and left him.

Back in her flat, depression hit her like a huge wave. She let it break over her, knowing there was nothing she could do—nothing. The future she had thought to have was gone. It could never return. Giles was gone—driven back up to Yorkshire to tell his parents she had called it off. She kept busy, cleaning her flat like one possessed. She had no appointments that day, which was just as well, as she could face no one—not even her booker.

She was signed with a different agency from the one where she had started her career as Kat Jones. This one had branches all over the world—all over the U.K. Even in Manchester.

That was where she had gone when Angelos Petrakos had destroyed her the first time around. She had gone there with Katya, both of them making a new life for themselves. They'd worked as cleaners—menial work to pay the rent, to eat, to survive. More than that had been beyond her. All she'd been able to bring herself to do was just keep going—nothing more than that. Then Katya had met a fellow Pole, Marek, to whom Katya was not just scar tissue, and who had said only one thing when Kat had told him how Mike had met his end—'He got lucky.'

Kat had seen the murderous look in Marek's eyes and known that Katya was safe now. She'd been happy for Katya—but when she'd gone she'd sat alone in their bedsit and stared at the walls.

They had started to move in on her. Slowly, inexorably, crushing the air out of the room, the breath out of her lungs, the life out of her veins. Shabby walls in a grimy flat on a grim street in a rundown part of the city where she spent her days as an office char, cleaning up other people's dirt.

Well, what do you expect? Two generations of losers, and you're the third. You tried to get out— and you lost. Accept it. You're not going anywhere any more. You're in the pit—so make yourself at home. It's where you belong, Kat Jones.

Then, out of the depths, the thought had come. *But I don't have to be Kat Jones…*

She'd sat very still as the thought had formed in her head. Formed and shaped and grown.

I can be someone else. I can be anyone I choose. Anyone.

But it wasn't just a name she'd needed. If all she'd taken was a new name Kat Jones would still have been underneath. She'd needed to be a new person. Someone a million miles away from Kat Jones—raised in care, daughter and grand-daughter of prostitutes, alcoholics and junkies. In her mind's eye she'd seen the sleek, glossy models who had been chosen by Angelos Petrakos. Not like her—with her Estuary English and her abrasive style and her pig-ignorance. But well-bred, well-spoken, well-behaved, well-educated.

Classy.

There had been a strange light in her eye. A burning light.

It was one that had lit her way through the years ahead.

Could that light still burn now, even through the dark, dark shadow of Angelos Petrakos? She knew there was only one answer she must give.

Yes. *Yes.* She could survive what he was doing to her—overcome it! She wasn't the raw, ignorant, penniless wannabe she'd been five years ago. She was Thea Dauntry, who owned a flat in Covent Garden, who had savings in the bank and a solid, well-paid career, who knew how to behave in the affluent, comfortable places of the world. Her rough London accent was smooth now, and cultured—as cultured as her mind had become through self-education, finally catching up on the years she had neglected at school.

Whatever Angelos Petrakos tried to do to her, he could not take that away. She was Thea Dauntry— and Kat Jones was gone for ever!

Yet, for all her resolution, it was hard—hideously hard—to pack an overnight case, lock her flat, and make her way, as she had been ordered, to his hotel. The same one, with vicious mockery, he had been staying at five long years ago—the same suite always reserved for him whenever he wanted to be in London.

Heart as heavy as lead, her mind studiedly, deliberately blank, she stepped inside the hotel, inside the revolving doors where, five long years ago, she had first set eyes on Angelos Petrakos. The man she hated with all her being and always would…

Angelos stared at the screen of his laptop. He wasn't reading what was on it—his thoughts

were elsewhere. Doing something they rarely
did. Questioning himself. A frown creased his
brow. Why was he doing this? Why should he care
whether some unknown man ended up married
to the likes of Kat Jones? He'd finished with her
five years ago…

There was no need to do what he was doing.

No need to bring her here again.

His expression shifted minutely. Need was not
the only driver for his decision, he knew. Something else was impelling him.

It was anger, that was all, he told himself. Anger
that she was set on deceiving an innocent, trusting
man who did not deserve it. Anger that she had
dared to do so and saw nothing wrong in doing
so. That was the only reason he was doing this.

He would allow it to be for no other reason.

*Not because of her luminous beauty that drew
the eye disturbingly…evocatively…*

The soft tones of the house phone sounded. He
glanced at his watch. The watch she had once
stolen from him. Two minutes to nine. He picked
up the phone. It was Reception. Kat Jones was
right on time.

Thea was calm. She would not allow herself to
be anything else. She was in lockdown. It was es-

sential. Essential in order to be able to walk into the suite, to see Angelos Petrakos again. She stood quite still, like a statue, staring ahead while the bellboy set down her case and then left. Angelos was looking at her, she could see. She would not look at him. But she could feel his presence like a dark pressure all around her.

'So…' his voice incised into the silence, deep and accented '…have you given your lordling his release?'

'Yes.' Her voice was dead. Unemotional.

'Good. Well, by tomorrow morning he will be permanently safe from you—even if you reneged on your rejection of him and went after him again he would have no wish to take my mistress for his wife, would he?'

'No.' The same deadness was in her voice.

He paused. Then in measured tones he spoke again. 'I am glad, Kat, that you understand that. There is no going back for you. Your ambitions in that direction are over. Permanently.'

He walked away from her, and from her eyeline she could see him cross to a drinks cabinet on the far side of the lavishly appointed suite. A terrifying surge of *déjà vu* suddenly swept over her, as if time had collapsed and she was once more standing here in that nightmare confrontation five years ago.

No! The lockdown on her mind tightened. No memories. *None.*

She made her eyes rest on him as he reached for a bottle and unstoppered it. She made herself look at him. Tall, powerful—brutal. Incised features, hard body, dark tanned skin, the darker hue of his black hair, the blacker shade of his hand-made business suit—all created the aura he was projecting. Not a man to mess with, not a man to defy—not a man to cross.

A man she could only…survive.

'What would you like to drink?'

The casual enquiry seemed at odds with the reality of the situation. As if there was anything sociable, anything *normal* in what she was doing here. Not like the grim, harsh truth of the situation.

'Mineral water,' she answered. Her voice was clipped. It sounded unreal, even to her, and she knew that she could still feel the shades of her once-rough accents haunting her. But that was Kat—and she was no longer Kat. She was Thea, and Thea spoke with pure Queen's English. No one looked down on her socially any more.

'Still or sparkling?'

'I couldn't care less,' she replied indifferently.

He finished pouring and then came back towards her, a tumbler of malt whisky in one hand, a tall glass of mineral water in the other. She set her handbag down on the coffee table and took the glass he proffered. She still didn't want to look at him, but she forced herself. She must not let him *see* she did not want to look at him. That would give him a satisfaction she must deny him. He would get nothing from her—no reaction at all.

Angelos Petrakos raised his tumbler.

'To our time together,' he said, and took a mouthful of the whisky. His eyes washed over her.

Thea's mouth suddenly felt dry as bone. She wanted to drink, wanted to drop her eyes away from him. But she forced herself to do neither— forced herself to let him look. She was used to being looked at—it was her profession, hate it though she did.

Did he see it in her eyes? He must have. Suddenly his eyes narrowed, as if she had done something to surprise him. Or remind him.

'You still don't like it, do you?' he observed. 'You don't like being looked at.' He took another, ruminative mouthful of his whisky. 'It was what

I noticed about you when you auditioned for the Monte Carlo campaign. That you don't like being looked at.' His expression changed minutely, and it seemed to Thea that his stance eased. 'Curious,' he said.

His eyes rested again on her face. She schooled her expression to be immobile, feeling the muscles in her body tighten. *Stop looking at me!* she wanted to scream at him.

He could see her tension, snapping from her like static. Felt himself respond to it. Immediately he clamped it down. If there was one thing he must not do it was respond to her! Yet memory crowded him, vivid and searing. She had stood just there, in that very spot.

Offering me her body. Letting me touch her, caress her...kiss her.

Like a guillotine falling, he cut the memory. With a jerking movement, he tossed the last of the whisky down, then replaced the tumbler on the tray.

'Let's go.'

She stared.

'Dinner,' he elaborated. 'To show the world you are keeping me company. That is, after all, your purpose here.'

She made no rejoinder to his sardonic remark, merely setting down her untouched glass and picking up her handbag. Stiffly she followed him from the room. She had dressed neutrally, in an aubergine-coloured dress that would do in most situations. Her hair was in its customary chignon, her make-up subdued.

Déjà vu was hitting her over and over again. Following Angelos Petrakos down to the hotel dining room was what she had done five years ago, but this time she was not fazed by her surroundings. She took them in her stride, along with the attentiveness of the waiters, murmuring her thanks and picking up her menu. She glanced down it with confidence—these days to her French menus were not incomprehensible and daunting. She glanced around. The décor was the same. Angelos Petrakos was the same. But she—she was different. Kat Jones had been ignorant—fatally ignorant. Oh, not of wine waiters and French menus. But of something that had proved her total undoing.

A strange look came into Thea's eye.

What if I'd just slapped him when he came on to me that nightmare night? Somehow dragged myself out of that zombie state he reduced me to when he kissed me and slapped him so hard that even he, in his colossal arrogance, would have got the message. That I wasn't, wasn't, wasn't 'leading him on'?

Would it have saved her? she wondered.

No—his monstrous ego would have taken offence at that, as well. He would never have given me that job back. I'd have been thrown out all the same, whatever I'd done.

Whatever I hadn't done...

Bitterness was like gall in her throat.

The waiter was hovering, and she made her selection. 'The grilled sole, please, with a green salad.'

'Is that all you intend to eat?' Angelos Petrakos's harsh tones cut across the table.

'Yes,' she replied. She said nothing more as he gave his own order, followed by a discussion with the sommelier. Then his eyes came back to her. She endured his surveillance.

'You're not as thin,' he remarked.

'These days I can afford food,' she said.

'Looking for sympathy, Kat?' he drawled.

'From *you*?' she returned scathingly.

'Still the mouth,' he observed. 'Do you really never learn, Kat?'

'Only the important things. But then, I had a

good teacher,' she said. Her eyes were like poison darts.

'But then,' he echoed deliberately, 'you were in urgent need of a lesson...'

She felt her anger rise, felt it heat her veins—and then, with absolute control, she forced it down. She reached for her water.

'Still no wine?'

'No.'

His eyes rested on her. 'Still the appearance of virtue. Did it help you reel in your captive lordling? How *did* you meet him?' he asked conversationally.

'It's none of your business and I won't discuss him with you.'

Angelos stilled. 'Your nerve is breathtaking.'

Thea set down her water with a jolt. 'You don't *really* imagine,' she bit out, 'that I care a fig about what I say to you, do you? I won't discuss Giles with you, period. He's a good, decent man, and because of you I've had to hurt him badly!'

His eyes darkened. 'Better that than marrying *you*!'

Emotion bit. She could feel it in her throat. It should be anger—anger at yet another insult. But it wasn't anger.

'I'd have made him a good wife,' she said tightly. Too tightly—as if her throat had suddenly narrowed. She felt a sudden ludicrous sting in the back of her eyes at his naked contempt. Even as it happened she fought it. She wouldn't, *wouldn't* feel what she did—she wouldn't feel, dear God, of all things, *hurt.*

She fought it back—fought it down. Recovered herself in the way she always had. By refusing to let anyone put her down. Refusing to acknowledge the hit.

Her imperviousness seemed only to rile him more.

'All that classy gloss, Kat,' he said softly, a taunt in his eyes, 'and it's all just fake. A cultivated act. A veneer. You'd never have carried it off—you'd have given yourself away, reverted to type.'

His eyes were resting on her, speculative, assessing. And suddenly, through the tightness in her throat, Thea could see what he was doing. He wanted to see her do just that—'revert to type'. And in that instant she knew exactly how she would retaliate from now on.

By not retaliating. By being Thea, not Kat—never Kat. She felt a surge of venomous satisfaction go through her.

'Nothing to say, Kat?'

She made no answer. Just tightened her lips and stared back at him. His eyes held hers—dark, penetrating. They narrowed very slightly even as he held her gaze.

'You defy me, don't you, Kat?' It was said almost contemplatively, almost curiously, as if she were a species of insect that was behaving anomalously. He took another leisurely mouthful of wine. 'But then,' he continued in that same tone of voice, 'you always did, didn't you? Right from that very first encounter, when you pushed past me at the entrance to this very hotel...' He set the glass back down on the linen tablecloth. 'Tell me, is it stupidity that makes you like this?'

Thea's fingers curled around her water glass. One tightening more and it would surely break. She resisted. She tilted her chin slightly, feeling the pearl drop earrings move slightly—pearls she had bought with her own money, her own efforts, her own relentless determination and hard work to achieve what she had. Climbing up from the nothing she had been born with into the sunlit lands above.

'No,' she answered, her voice deliberately careless. 'It's indifference, that's all. Complete indifference.'

The expression on his face changed. Something flashed in his eyes, then it was gone. She had seen what it was, though—anger. Oh, yes, the almighty Angelos Petrakos, with all his power, didn't like being told that!

He spoke again, his deep voice almost a drawl. A drawl that seemed to drag across her skin. 'Indifference? Oh, no, Kat. It's not indifference you feel towards me. It's anger because you can't manipulate me.'

Her eyes flashed, and Angelos felt a stab of satisfaction. He *wanted* her angry, lashing out at him. Breaking the surface of the smooth, flawless veneer she had plastered over her true nature.

Because that was what it was—he would allow it to be nothing else. Nothing more...

'Angelos! Darling! I had no idea you were in London!'

The scent of heavy perfume wafted across the table and Thea turned her head to see someone approaching that she recognised. Not that she knew her personally, but because the woman bearing down upon them was a well-known TV actress who specialised in the *femme fatale* roles for which her dramatic looks were well suited. Thea watched Angelos acknowledge the woman's greeting, but though his expression was impassive she could see irritation in the back of his eyes.

'Candice,' he said briefly.

The actress's eyes rested on his face avidly for a moment, then gave the briefest glance in Thea's direction. For an instant they were blank—then there was a flash of malice.

'Don't you usually run around with Giles Brooke? Be careful, my dear, or you may find the Viscountess's coronet slipping through your fingers!'

'It was never mine to let slip.' Thea gave a courteous smile, ignoring the jibe.

Arched eyebrows rose. 'No? It looked like you had him wrapped around your finger?'

'I wouldn't really have fitted the bill as his wife, Miss Paule.' Thea's voice was subdued.

The actress breathed out, the malice in her eyes even more pronounced. 'So he didn't propose after all? Oh, my *dear*, I'm so sorry!' Her insincerity was masterly. Her voice became conspiratorial. 'No wonder you've decided to settle for more transient pleasures. Enjoy them—on Angelos's established record they will be so *very* transient!

Now, Angelos darling—' her tone was now cajoling '—I must introduce you to someone I'm here with. He's got the most fascinating project planned. He wants me to play the lead as soon as the finance is sorted. It's going to be a sure-fire hit, and if you came in on it you'd absolutely clean up—'

'TV and film isn't my investment area, Candice,' said Angelos bluntly, cutting across her.

For a moment the actress's expression faltered. 'Oh, but surely since it's me who's involved you'd make an exception—'

'Candice, I made it crystal clear during our time together that our relationship was personal, not professional. I don't mix the two. Ever.'

The over-made-up eyes flashed. 'Better make sure Little Miss Jilted knows that! She'll be assuming she's a dead cert for your next advertising campaign just because she's warming your bed!' she snapped, and flounced off back to her party.

Thea watched her go. Then she became aware that Angelos was watching her.

'That's a lesson you've already learned,' he said softly. Then, abruptly, his expression changed. 'Why didn't you set Candice right about the assumption she made that Brooke never proposed to you? She'll spill it to the first gossip columnist she sees.'

'I know,' said Thea. 'That's why I told her.'

Angelos's brows drew together. 'What are you plotting?' he demanded.

Thea looked straight at him. 'I've hurt Giles—you gave me no option but to do so—but I don't want to humiliate him. I'd rather it looked like he didn't want to marry me than that I ditched him for *you.*'

Her mouth twisted, and he felt a stab of something more than anger.

The arrival of their food distracted him, but as they started to eat he found himself watching her. She was filleting the fish, focussing on her task. Blanking him out.

He made himself recall how she had looked that first evening he had brought her here. How gauche she had been, how out of her depth. The woman sitting opposite him now was a million miles from the one she had been those years ago.

She's still Kat Jones—thief, liar, and ready to offer her body for what she wants...

His mouth tightened. That was all he must remember.

* * *

By the time the meal was finally over and they were heading for the elevators Thea's nerves were at breaking point. There were others in the lift when they stepped in, and Thea was grateful. Being alone with Angelos Petrakos, even for the briefest time, was hideous. Sitting at the same table as him—being so physically close to his lean, powerful body, sheathed in its charcoal bespoke suit, seeing that strong-featured face with its short-clipped raven hair, the dark, glinting eyes and the sensual, brutal mouth—had overwhelmed her. Even in the dining room she had felt dangerously isolated with him, despite the presence of other diners.

The elevator doors sliced opened to let some people out and others in. Too many. They hustled her backwards and suddenly, without realising what was about to happen, she felt herself crushed back against Angelos. Shock at his sudden closeness immobilised her. It raked through her as she felt instantly, consummately, the hardness of his chest, the muscle of his thigh.

Behind her, Angelos felt the contours of her body mould against him, slender and rounded. Immediately his hands lifted to her shoulders, steadying her. She tensed instantly. His palms were burning as he felt her straining away from him, pulling against his hands. Automatically, instinctively, his hold tightened, countering her attempt to free herself.

The lift stopped again and she wrenched free, pushing her way out, stalking rapidly to the door of his suite, body rigid. Her spine was like a ramrod. The contact had lasted only moments, but it had ignited her overwrought nerves, exploded the iron control she had held down all evening.

Inside, she rounded on him. Her face was contorted, venom spitting from her eyes. 'Don't touch me! Don't *ever* touch me!'

Into her head sliced the forbidden memory—the one she never let out! The one that for five long years she had never, *ever* let herself remember. But here in this place, this very spot where it had happened, here where she was standing, now it flooded through her.

I stood here—here! And he came up to me and... and...

Hot, humid memory drenched her. The glide of his fingertips touching her, the deep, deep drowning of his mouth as it moved on hers, sensual, possessing...

A shudder went through her—through every

bone in her body, every cell. 'I couldn't *bear* it!' she said. She took a ragged, broken breath. 'This is a two-bedroom suite—I checked!' She dived on her small holdall, snatching it up. Then—not looking at him again, not looking anywhere near him—she flung open the nearest door leading off the suite's lounge.

It wasn't his room. Unoccupied, empty. She plunged inside and slammed shut the door, leaning against it while the breath shook in her body.

Outside, Angelos stood immobile. Emotion was raging through his head. Emotion that he'd kept out by strength of will, by masking it with anger. Anger that he'd deliberately, determinedly fuelled since the moment he'd first set eyes on her again at that restaurant with the man she'd been inveigling to marry, slicing back through the years—anger that he'd used deliberately, determinedly, to allow him to do what he had done in summoning her here. Giving him a reason to force her back into his life—a reason to sever her from the man she'd wanted to marry. He'd been telling himself that he was doing so only because he was enraged by her attempt to lie about her past, to fool an innocent, hapless man about what she truly was.

But he'd been deceiving himself.

Anger was *not* the only driving force behind his determination to stop Kat Jones in her tracks. He'd been denying that truth all through dinner as he'd watched her across the table from him, seeing her graceful, elegant beauty drawing eyes as it always had—and his, too, he knew. Despite everything he felt about her he could not deny that—could not deny that his eyes wanted to rest on her, take in that extraordinary, luminous beauty of hers...

Then, in the lift, his hands closing over her shoulders, his palms feeling the warmth of her body, catching the scent of her, her body so close to his, it had blazed in him. He had known then, irrefutably, what her power was...what it had always been...

A power she herself was trying to deny.

In his head shrilled her voice, loathing and fear in it—*'Don't touch me! Don't ever touch me! I couldn't bear it!'*

His face twisted, new emotion working in him.

She hates you for what you did to her. It dominates her response to you, obliterating everything else.

Slowly, he walked into his bedroom, his mind still full. He had done what he had to her five long years ago because there had been no other way to impose justice upon her—because she had outwit-ted the law with her lies and slander. He felt no remorse for what he had done—why should he? She had stolen from him, slandered him—and got away with it in the eyes of the law.

But she had not got away with it in *his* eyes—he knew the truth of what she had done—and so he had exacted his own justice upon her. Just as, now, he'd refused to allow her to continue to deceive her hapless fiancé about her past.

But she's paid the price for both...

Did he need to feel only anger towards her any more? Or was he now free to indulge that other, equally powerful emotion he felt about her? The one that was even more powerful now, five years on, in the face of her new, mature, cultured beauty.

He didn't know. Not clearly yet. Knew only, as his hand went with automatic gestures to loosen his tie as he proceeded to head for his solitary bed, in the acute consciousness of her presence so short a distance away, that he wanted to find out—and that to do so would require continuing to keep her with him.

But not here. His thoughts resolved themselves, gelling to a point of decision that focused within him with sudden clarity. He did not want to be here with her, in this suite, with the memory of how she had behaved five years ago all around him, dragging him back into the past. No—if he was to allow himself to feel any emotion for her other than anger, as that revelatory moment in the elevator had forced him to admit he did, then he must take her somewhere he could discover the truth of her character, whatever she called herself now.

And he knew exactly the place.

Decision made, he started to ready himself for bed. From tomorrow he would start to discover the truth he was seeking. And whether he could have what he wanted.

CHAPTER SIX

SOMEONE was knocking softly. Thea heard the sound of a door opening, then a female voice spoke.

'Madam, breakfast is served.'

Blearily, Thea raised her head from the pillow. She had scarcely slept—not until dawn had been fingering across the city sky. Her head had been filled with memories—memories she had fought for five years.

I let him—I let him kiss me. I did not fight, I did not yell, or pull away, or hit at him, or anything—anything at all. I just stood there and let him do that to me...

But now, at last, the day had come—her release. She was free, she thought blankly, to go home, take up her empty life again.

Swiftly, she made a basic *toilette*, desperate to be gone. But as she walked out of her bedroom her eyes immediately fell on him, fully dressed in a business suit, seated at the breakfast table.

There was no sign of the maid who had roused her. His head turned as she came into the room. For a moment their eyes met, then she blanked hers and said, her tone brisk, 'I'm going now.'

His expression did not change. 'You're going nowhere. Come here, Kat, and sit down. I may not keep my mistresses long, but I keep them longer than one night. You're coming with me to Geneva—we leave at noon.'

Her dismay was open. 'I can't just leave London. I have appointments.' It was all she could think to say through the tide of rejection sweeping through her at his words.

'Cancel them,' he said indifferently. 'Your agency can phone my office if there are any problems. I'll compensate for any contractual objections arising from your absence.'

She stood, fulminating with fury—and something more than fury that was not fear, never fear, but still made her want to rush from the room. But if she did his threat to expose her to Giles would hang over her head still…

She set her face. She could not let Angelos see either her fury or her dismay. 'You said noon, I believe?' she said carelessly.

He nodded.

'Very well.' She didn't bother to ask what she should pack. Didn't bother to do anything except head for the door and leave.

At the table, Angelos watched her go. Was he deranged? Deranged to do this? Yet one glimpse of her standing there, bristling and defiant, her face bare of make-up yet still startlingly beautiful, had told him that his decision was the right one. Definitely the right one. Whatever he wasn't sure about, one thing *was* for sure—he was not about to let Kat Jones go.

The executive jet skimmed the cloud surface. Sunlight poured in through Thea's porthole. How could the world be so bright when inside her head was only darkness? Across the aisle Angelos sat, ensconced in paperwork. Her mask of studied indifference had hardly been needed. He had ignored her presence throughout the journey to the airfield and so far throughout the flight. His attention had been reserved only for his work—and the smiling stewardess who had fawned over him. Thea would have laughed at her efforts had she not had a stone in her chest. She stared, unseeing, down at her book, taking in nothing.

How was she to get through what was to come?

And what *was* to come? The stone in her chest hardened.

If he tries it—if he lays a finger on me…

Panic choked her throat, and she fought it down, regaining control of herself. Keeping that control rigidly for the remainder of the flight, and then for the business of deplaning and travelling into the centre of Geneva. She was considerably better travelled now than she had been when she'd been Kat, but Geneva was new to her, and she gazed about her as a car drove them along the edge of Lac Lemain, past the famous iconic fountain jetting out of the water, and turned into the older part of town. The hotel was discreetly expensive, and Kat felt panic bite again as they were shown into Angelos's suite. It subsided again as the bellboy took her bag into a separate bedroom. Surely if Angelos intended to try and get her into bed he would not have allowed her a bedroom of her own?

But if that was not his intent—then what was? The question ran round the inside of her skull, finding no answer, only tormenting her.

Her tension still sky-high, she heard Angelos's voice from the doorway.

'I have engagements this afternoon. Do whatever you want, but be ready to go to dinner at eight.'

She looked at him stiffly, stifling her anxieties, making herself think only of trivial, practical things. 'What dress code?'

'Cocktail,' he said briefly. 'And, Kat, this is Switzerland. They're a sober people. Dress accordingly.'

The outfit she'd chosen, out of the variety she had brought with her must have been what he had in mind, for he made no comment on the knee-length olive-green dress. Her nerves were stretched like wire. She had spent the afternoon desultorily watching television and reading, and somehow she would get through the evening. She was relieved to find they were not *à deux*, as she had dreaded, but instead at a dinner function held in a private dining room at an expensive restaurant. She had gone into the kind of automatic social chitchat she was used to with Giles, and had it not been for Angelos Petrakos's brooding presence would have found the experience perfectly pleasant.

She did her best to ignore Angelos, but his was not an easy presence to ignore. She was conscious all the time of his deep voice, his harsh, handsome features, and the dominating impact he made at the table, drawing the eyes, she knew, of all the other women present. At one point towards the end of the evening, to her shock, she heard him laugh—a sound she had never heard before. Her head whipped round, and she could only blink as she saw how the planes of his face had altered completely, with deep lines indenting around his mouth. She felt a jolt go through her, and for one fatal moment his line of sight intercepted hers. The jolt came again, like an electric shock, then, draggingly, she tore her eyes away.

It had shaken her—and as she got back into the limo she knew her tension was sky-high again. Yet Angelos did not speak to her until, back in the suite, he turned to her. She was standing, not sure what to do, in the middle of the room.

'It's really quite remarkable,' he said. His eyes rested on her. 'If I didn't know the truth about you I would be as fooled as anyone. You're unrecognisable from five years ago.'

He flicked his dark gaze up and down her, as she stood, immobile, making her face expressionless. Then he turned away, and she felt her muscles sag in reaction.

'I've work to do,' he said dismissively. 'Tomorrow you can do what you wish, but we need to leave for the concert hall by seven. Dress code is black tie.'

She took her dismissal, and escaped to the refuge of her bedroom.

Against all her expectations, Thea slept well. Maybe she was just compensating for the previous sleepless night. When she woke it was already ten o'clock. Tentatively she ventured from her room. There was no sign of Angelos, and no sound from his room. After a while she relaxed, knowing he was not there. Nevertheless, she dressed swiftly and left the hotel. It was a dull morning, threatening rain, and she took coffee and a roll for breakfast in a café. Her mood was strange. She seemed remote, dissociated from herself and the rest of the world—dissociated, too, from memories of Giles, the man she had thought she was going to marry but who now seemed as unreal as if she had dreamt him.

She spent the rest of the day exploring Geneva, walking along the lake's edge. A slight wind was ruffling the surface of the dark water. Finding an unoccupied bench, she sat down, looking out over the lake, at the clouds scudding overhead.

This is an interlude in my life. Nothing more. It's

a question of getting through the days, reaching the end. I don't know when the end will be, but it will come. At some point he will let me go. Until then—I must wait. Just wait.

For a moment longer she looked out, unblinking, out across the lake. Then, with an intake of breath, as if to mark a decision to think no more for now, she opened her bag and got out her book to read—a pocket history of the city.

She got back to the hotel in good time, bathed and dressed herself. Then emerged from her room a few minutes before seven. Angelos was already there.

Her eyes went to him immediately, as they always did. But now, as she looked at him, she felt her breath catch—hate herself though she did for it. She had never seen him in evening dress before. It made any man look good, she knew. But on a man like Angelos Petrakos it was—breathtaking. The stark formality of the tuxedo, the dazzling white of the shirt sheathing his powerful frame, contrasting with the black bow tie, was devastating in its impact. She felt it jolting through her, rendering her incapable of doing anything but staring at him, taking him in. Feeling his power...

He'd been talking on his mobile, but he finished

his call, turning to inspect her. She held herself rigidly steady, refusing to react to him.

'Another elegant outfit,' he murmured, eyes flickering over the black silk evening trousers topped with a long-waisted, long-sleeved silk jacket faintly threaded with silver. Tonight she was not wearing pearls, but a filigree silver necklace that fitted into the narrow vee between the revers of her jacket, and long, graceful silver earrings. Her hair, as ever, was in its customary chignon.

'Models get discounts,' she said carelessly, stepping into the elevator.

He made no reply, and they travelled down in silence, but Thea was aware of his gaze on her. Aware, too, of his presence at her side, of the faint tang of aftershave and, deeper than that, of a shivering sense of his raw, ruthless masculinity.

It persisted, to her growing discomfort, through the evening ahead. All through the concert as she sat beside him—too close, far, far too close!—she could feel his presence there. Feel the heat of his body, the long line of his leg so close to hers, feel his shoulder almost graze hers. She kept her hands doggedly in her lap, not using the armrest at all lest her arm brush against the smooth, svelte sleeve of his dinner jacket.

But though she was not touching him he was there all the same. Far too close. Far too real. Doggedly, she determined to concentrate only on the music. To appreciate the opportunity to listen to a world-famous orchestra, see a world-famous conductor and soloist, in acoustically the best seats in the house.

She wished, though, it had not been Rachmaninov. The lush, lavish tones of the second symphony poured over her, disturbing her senses, arousing her emotions. She felt its power dissolving her rigidly imposed control. The music seemed to strip it away, making her feel things she did not want to feel. Arousing emotions she did not want aroused. She sought to hold herself immobile in her seat, spine straight, hands still, but the music swayed through her, crescendo after crescendo. And always the perpetual consciousness of the dark, disturbing presence of Angelos Petrakos at her side.

The second half of the concert was Shostakovich, and all the lushness of Rachmaninov was swept away in stormy discordance. She was glad of that, too. But when the concert finally ended it appeared their evening was not yet over. Angelos made his way with her up to a spacious private function VIP salon, where there was some kind of reception going on. Just as he had the night before, Angelos introduced her to whoever he talked to, and Thea found herself in the same kind of social situation. She performed her allotted role perforce, discussing the concert or any other subject that came up, sipping sparkling mineral water and orange juice, allowing herself a little of the delicious-looking buffet.

But if the polyglot social-chitchat was easy enough, coping with Angelos's constant presence at her side was not.

It seemed to be getting worse, her consciousness of him.

He was standing far too close to her. The space was crowded, with groups forming and breaking up, waiters circling with trays of drinks and canapés, and she felt his body always too close to hers, felt herself oppressed by his nearness whenever his sleeve brushed her arm or once—worst of all, and making her spine freeze—when his hand grazed the small of her back to draw her aside and let a waiter come by. She knew there was nothing she could do—they were in a social setting, and she could not react by pulling sharply away, biting out at him vehemently. Instead she had to continue smiling, conversing, being polite, courteous, civil, as the occasion warranted.

And all the time beneath the surface she felt like a radio receiver set to maximum—and to a single frequency. Hyper awareness of Angelos— his presence, his voice, his occasional low laugh that seemed to vibrate somewhere very deep in her bones, a disturbing, debilitating frisson.

It worsened on the way back to the hotel, in the confines of the limo, though she did her best to stare out of the window.

'Did you really enjoy the concert, or were you merely mouthing politely?'

The question made her head turn. In the shadowy light the strong planes of Angelos's features seemed more overpowering than ever.

'Why should you want to know?' she countered.

'I'm curious about you,' he answered. His eyes rested on her in the dim light.

His scrutiny disturbed her. 'I can't possibly like classical music?' she riposted sarcastically.

'The Kat Jones I knew would not.'

She gave a half-shrug. 'That's why I became Thea. No one,' she went on, and found her voice had tightened, 'should be Kat Jones. No one should be that ignorant, that uneducated.'

'So why *were* you? Ignorant and uneducated? Schooling is free in Britain.'

She gave another shrug. 'You can lead a horse to water… I was like far too many children from that background. I simply thought my teachers were trying to control me, and everything they tried to teach me seemed pointless, stupid and boring. I wouldn't play their game, and I thought that made me smarter than those docile morons who did.'

Why was she saying this? she thought. Why tell him anything? Why talk to him? Why acknowledge his existence? Yet she was, all the same, though she did not know why.

'What changed you?'

She looked at him. 'You did,' she said.

There was a moment's silence. Then she spoke again.

'You destroyed Kat Jones. So I stopped being her.'

The dark, long-lashed eyes narrowed. 'Did you, Kat?'

'Yes. And if you destroy Thea Dauntry I'll become someone else. Because you'll never destroy *me*. I won't let you. Whatever you do to me, I'll survive it. I'll survive everything. I'll survive *you.*'

Her eyes held his. Held them and would not back down. The car travelled on, turning a wide corner, and her gaze broke.

Why on earth did I say that? What for?

Her eyes looked out at the anonymous rain-wet streets. What was she doing here, in this city she did not know, with the man who was her persecutor? Why had the twists and turns of her life brought her here, to this moment, to this man? Her eyes flicked back to him. He was looking at her, and she broke the gaze again. But his image stayed imprinted, shadowy, disturbing, on her retina.

Why this man?

The words echoed in her head. *Why this man?*

But she did not know the answer.

Her dreams that night were confused, disturbing, filled with the lush, impassioned strains of Rachmaninov. She woke, music still echoing in her ears, to find sunshine pouring into the room and Angelos still in the suite, breakfasting. Stiffly, she took her place, shaking out a pristine white napkin over her lap and reaching for the freshly squeezed orange juice. As she poured her juice it registered on her that he was not wearing his customary business suit. Instead he was wearing a grey cashmere sweater, and it made him look, she realised, with yet another jangle to her stretched nerves, disturbingly different from his usual power-suited self.

Before she could wonder why he wasn't in a suit, he spoke. 'Today,' he announced, as he poured himself a refill of coffee, 'we shall be leaving Geneva. I'd like to get going right after breakfast, so please ensure you are packed.'

She only nodded, refusing to ask where their next destination was. High powered business types like him, she knew, travelled the world constantly, and presumably yet another private jet would be waiting for him this morning.

But when they exited the hotel, waiting at the kerb was not the customary smoked-glass-windowed limo, but a sleek, low, powerful, luxury high-performance car. The doorman hurried to open the passenger door for her, and the parking valet to open the driver's door for Angelos. Thea lowered herself in warily. What was going on? Where were they going? But she would not ask, and Angelos did not enlighten her even when they

were clear of the city and its environs on a road
that seemed to be heading decidedly towards the
mountains.

So she merely sat still as they climbed steadily
up increasingly tortuous roads into the mountains.
Snow still capped their peaks, glistening in the
brilliant sun which turned the Alpine pastures
to verdant green and the pine forests to a dark
lustre, transformed the rushing streams that the
road crossed in its climb to sparkling diamonds.
Watching the dramatic scenery gave her something to do—something to distract her from Angelos's presence. Yet from the corner of her eye
she could still see the strong curve of his hands on
the wheel, the glint of sun on the dark glasses he
had slid over his eyes. The sense of his presence
was, as ever, overpowering.

How long the journey took she didn't register,
but it must have been a good couple of hours.
They'd driven through several towns, the last
one clearly a ski resort in winter, but now they
were leaving it behind and climbing up a narrow
road marked by snow poles, rising steeply into
the mountains towards a col that was visible in
the distance. Then, abruptly, the car turned off
even this road and started to snake slowly, with its

low suspension, up an unmetalled track towards a wide stand of pine trees about half a mile further ahead. Any sign of human habitation had been left far down in the valley.

As the car rounded the base of the stand of pine trees the unmetalled track opened out and revealed, cantilevered out over the steep slope of the mountainside, a large wooden chalet with a sharply angled roof and wrap-around wooden balconies at several levels. It was spectacularly sited—as if hanging on to the edge of the mountain. Angelos slewed the car to a halt near the entrance, which was bedecked with flower baskets full of trailing geraniums. Several people were issuing out of the chalet—a middle-aged man, a younger one and a maid.

Angelos cut the engine and got out of the car, greeting the older man in German and nodding at the younger members of staff. As Thea got out of the climate-controlled interior of the car she felt her lungs seize. The air was crystal, sharp and clear, the sunlight dazzling. She gazed about her, breathing deeply. The setting of the huge chalet was breathtaking, but she could only stare around her for the time it took for Angelos to ushered her forward, pausing briefly to introduce the staff to her. She smiled politely at them, glad that they seemed to speak fluent English. Indoors, as Thea looked around a large hall with a sweeping wooden staircase leading to the upper levels, was the kind of rustic luxury that only real wealth could afford. A huge fireplace with antlers on the wall above, everything wood-panelled, wood-floored, solid furniture gleaming with the patina of assiduous polishing, and warm rugs and carpets in abundance. Although the style was simple, it was clear a great deal of money had been spent on it. Yet nothing was ostentatious, and the overall effect was warm and appealing.

The maid took her upstairs, showing her into a spacious, sunny bedroom in the same solid, wood-dominated style, and Thea's eyes were drawn immediately to the doors leading out on to the balcony at this level. Thanking the maid, who had started to unpack for her, she wandered out.

The view was incredible! She had realised it must be spectacular, but actually standing here, poised over the edge of the mountain, it was as if she was almost a bird in flight, soaring down from the high peak. The clarity of the air caught at her lungs again, and as she gazed about the snow-capped peaks were impossible to look at in the brilliant sunshine. She wrapped her hands around the sun-warmed wood of the balustrade and gave a sigh of pleasure.

'Is that a vote in favour?'

A deep, half-drawling voice sounded from along the balcony, and Thea's head whipped round. Angelos had emerged from what she assumed must be the master bedroom, further along. He strolled towards her.

He was still wearing his sunglasses, and for the first time Thea was looking at him straight on. She felt a jab of dismay. Why, oh why, did sunglasses do for him what they were so obviously doing? And not just to him—to her...

'The view is amazing,' she said, her voice stiff, but she felt it would be unfair to the unknown architect of the chalet to deny it.

'You don't suffer from vertigo, I take it?' remarked Angelos.

She shook her head.

'Nevertheless,' he warned, 'do not lean over too far, and when you are outdoors be careful. The paths can be treacherous, with scree that's unstable, and it is easy to lose your balance if you too near to any sheer drops. Don't emulate the goats—they are bred to the mountains!' A half-smile tugged at his mouth, and Thea realised with a strange twist inside that it made his features less severe.

'You must be hungry after the drive. Lunch awaits us. Come.'

He led the way past her and down a level—the lower level of the balcony was linked to the upper by a flight of open-tread wooden stairs. The lower balcony was wider yet, almost a terrace, and a table with a red-checked tablecloth had been set out, laid for a meal. The manservant helped her to her seat, and she murmured, *'Danke,'* which was about all the German she knew, apart from *bitte.*

The manservant answered something in German which sounded odd.

'Switzerdeutsch,' said Angelos to Thea. 'Swiss-German. Don't even try and understand it! Even I find it very hard still.' He nodded a smile at the manservant, who said something in more normal-sounding German, to which Angelos responded, again with a smile.

It was weird to see him smile. Weird to see him without a business suit. Weird to see him with the sun glinting off his dark hair. The sun was still dazzling, and the manservant crossed to the wall and operated a mechanism which resulted in an awning extending to shield the sun from their eyes. Angelos kept his dark glasses on, all the same, and Thea realised it was making things slightly easier, not being able to see his eyes. The manservant was busy setting out drinks, opening a bottle of white wine, which, as usual, Thea refused with a polite smile.

She wanted to ask if the chalet was Angelos's, but why should she want to know? He probably owned properties all over the world. Rich people did. Instead, she found herself saying, 'How many languages do you speak?'

The moment she said it she wondered what had possessed her to ask a question—to show any sign of interest in him at all.

He did not seem to find her question out of place.

'Four,' he answered. 'Including Greek, of course. English is mandatory now, and I learnt both French and German while I was here in Switzerland at school.'

Thea stared. It was impossible to think of Angelos Petrakos as a schoolboy. Just impossible.

'You were brought up in Switzerland?' she found herself asking—and again immediately wondered

why she had asked. It was not an unreasonable
question. As Thea, she had come to know that
many wealthy people of many nationalities were
based in the financial haven of Switzerland.

'No, I was sent to boarding school here at thir-
teen. My father thought it a good idea to broaden
my horizons. Switzerland is full of international
schools offering an excellent education.'

'Didn't your mother mind you boarding?'

Questions were coming from her, and she didn't
know why. It could only be, she reasoned, because
she had gone into some kind of automatic social
behaviour more, assuming the kind of conversation that she was familiar with when she talked
to people. How else could she possibly be sitting
here, having the semblance of a normal conversation with him?

'She died when I was three. I don't remember
her. I was brought up by my father. We were very
close. I was his only child. But he spent his life
working, creating Petrakos International. Over-
working. He died when I was twenty-one.'

The clipped tones revealed nothing, and she
could not see his eyes. But she saw him lift his
wrist slightly.

'This watch was his twenty-first birthday present to me—the last gift he ever gave me. I've worn it every day since.' He paused, then said deliberately, 'So you will understand that its value is more than its cost...'

She felt colour run over her cheeks. 'I'm not proud of what I did,' she said in a low voice.

'So why did you?'

The question slipped in like a blade. In her mind's eye Thea saw the sick, silver glint of the blade in Mike's hand. She slammed the vision away. She would not think of that—would not think about Kat and what she had done. Why she had done it. It was over, gone—another life. A life she no longer led.

Would never lead again. Whatever Angelos Petrakos did to her.

She gave no answer, and was grateful that their food arrived at that moment. Surprised, too, by the quickening of her appetite as a rich, fragrant meat soup, sprinkled with herbs and enriched with dumplings, was set in front of her.

'You'd better get used to eating more,' observed Angelos. 'The mountain air is infamous for creating appetite.' He spoke as if he'd never mentioned that she'd stolen his father's last gift to him. Then he went on, 'Tell me, how are you at walking?'

Thea's spoon stayed in mid-lift.

'Mountain walks,' said Angelos. 'It's what I come here for.'

She stared. The picture of Angelos Petrakos walking over Swiss mountains was not an image she had thought it possible to entertain. How could he be the arrogant Mr Rich and Powerful with nothing around him but mountains?

'I haven't any walking boots,' she replied, for something to say.

'I've had a selection sent up from the village, and a range of suitable clothing.'

Well, that was being Mr Rich again, certainly, she allowed. But then, so was owning a spectacular chalet like this. Yet it still seemed out of keeping with what she knew about him.

But what do I know about him except that he destroys people who cross him?

That was all she needed to know about him.

Nothing else. Nothing about the person he might or might not be. Nothing about where he came from, or what his family had been to him, or his boyhood. Nothing.

And nothing, *nothing* at all, about the way her eyes wanted to go constantly to him, or the way she could feel his presence, as if she were an antenna, tuning to its frequency.

She dragged her eyes away, dropping them back to her soup bowl.

Angelos watched her from behind his dark glasses. Would she have answered his question had the food not arrived? Would she have attempted to justify her behaviour? Her words echoed—*'I'm not proud of what I did...'*

Another echo sounded, from the evening before. *'No one should be Kat Jones...'*

She had changed beyond recognition—except to him. But had she changed enough inside to hate what she'd done as Kat? The question hung in his mind, unanswered, as his gaze rested on her as she ate, taking in her grace, her extraordinary beauty that drew his eye so powerfully.

But one thing he knew. He had been right to bring her here. Here, up in the mountains, with the busy world left far, far behind, at this lofty elevation where the air was crystal, the light clearer, he would see the truth about her.

And the truth of what he wanted of her.

CHAPTER SEVEN

THEA paused a moment, flexing her calf muscles. Angelos was striding ahead of her. He was setting a fast pace, but Thea would not be hurried. She was still getting a feel for the boots, and since she had no idea how far he was expecting her to walk she knew she had to pace herself. They were on a pine-needle path snaking up through the fir trees that encircled the chalet on three sides, shielding it from view of the road far below, and the incline was already getting steeper. It was very quiet and dark in the perpetual shade of the conifers, and when the path led out on to the bare mountain slope she blinked in the dazzling sunlight. Ahead of her, Angelos had paused to put on sunglasses, and she did the same. Then, with nothing more than a glance back at her, he resumed walking.

Thea headed after him, keeping him in view but also gazing around her. It was impossible to do otherwise. The panorama was immense. The steep slope of the mountain side curved away to the road far below, getting further away all the time as they climbed upwards towards the ridge they were clearly heading for. After an hour or so of walking she could feel it in the backs of her legs. But she didn't care—the scenery around her was too glorious, the air in her lungs like cleansing crystal. She felt—even though she knew it was quite bizarre to feel this way, given why she was here and who she was with—a strange sense of peace.

It was impossible, here in the wide open air, so high above the world, to feel anything else.

After another half an hour she reached the ridge. Angelos had been there for some time, standing framed against the skyline, looking back down at her from time to time.

Angelos Petrakos on his lofty mountaintop, gazing down disdainfully at the common people struggling below...

She said nothing as she finally drew level with him. She was not exactly out of breath, but she knew she was feeling the exertion. He looked at her, eyes still invisible behind his dark lenses, and Thea was glad her eyes were similarly veiled.

'Think you can make it up there?'

He indicated a rocky outcrop, jagged against the

skyline, further along the ridge, which continued to rise until, way beyond, it ascended steeply up a bare rockface to begin a proper summit of the next mountain in the chain.

Thea shrugged, reaching for her water bottle and drinking deeply. Angelos was watching her impassively.

She'd done well so far, he allowed grudgingly. He'd set a deliberately fast pace, to see what she would do, but she'd just followed him. Doggedly, steadily. Now he studied her. Was it bravado that was keeping her going? He did not want to have to carry her down if she overdid it and collapsed.

'Tell me if you need to stop,' he said tersely, then he set off again.

Thea put her water away, took a breath, and went after him. The path was more difficult now, disappearing in places, and the ridge was getting narrower. But she kept going. Angelos did not outpace her now, deliberately, she assumed, slowing to her pace. There was a sharp wind, too, keening up the scarp slope they were now exposed to on the far side of the ridge. But walking had made her hot, and she was glad of its cooling.

Another half-hour of walking got them to the outcrop that he'd indicated. As they gained it Thea realised that the rocks it was made from framed a grassy hollow, looking out over the next valley. Angelos shrugged off his rucksack and levered himself down on to the close-cropped turf.

'Sit down,' he ordered.

Reluctantly, for the grassy hollow was not large, Thea did as she was bade, keeping the maximum distance from him she could. Unfortunately, with his broad shoulders and their thick jumpers, that was not much. Worse, out of the wind but still in the sun, and glowing from her exertion, she felt far too hot.

'Take off the jumper,' said Angelos, and proceeded to remove his.

Again reluctantly, Thea did as she was bade, feeling immediate relief to be only in the flannel shirt beneath.

'Now drink more water,' Angelos instructed, extracting his own flask once more.

Again, Thea did likewise, and felt the cool water snake down her parched throat.

'Worth the climb?' Angelos enquired laconically as she lowered the flask to her lap. Her legs, like his, were stretched out straight, but angled away from him.

She gazed around, taking in the splendours of

this high, lonely place. All around mountains stretched as far as the eye could see, their peaks snow-capped, their sides verdant. Below her the ridge dropped down into a deep valley, uninhabited from what she could see.

It was as if they had the world to themselves.

As if they were the only people in it.

She didn't answer, only sat, glad of the rest, while her gaze took in the vast space all around. Apart from the keening of the wind there was no noise. Sun burned down on her, and she was glad of her dark glasses. Her skin felt hot, and she dipped into her pocket for her sun cream, methodically working it over her face to renew its protection.

Beside her, Angelos watched her. She was absorbed in her task, still gazing out ahead of her. She was paying him no attention, but it didn't bother him. He wanted to watch her. Study her.

Yet again she was different. The groomed, soignée Thea he'd seen for the past few days had changed. But it was not just in appearance, with the functional climbing gear and her hair snaking down her back in a plait to resist the wind, but in the way she sat there. Gazing out quietly. She put the sun cream away and tucked her legs up, hooking her arms loosely around her knees, face lifted as she looked about her.

'That peak there is the Hohenhorn,' he heard himself saying, indicating the tallest mountain in the direction she was looking. 'Below us the Heinser valley. The drop is nearly a thousand metres.'

Suddenly she felt her shoulder brushed. Automatically she stiffened, but Angelos's deep voice only said, 'Look—there—hanging below the Hohenhorn—a pair of eagles!'

She swivelled her head, staring, trying to make out the specks his outstretched arm was pointing at.

'I see them!' she exclaimed. She watched, riveted, as the pair twisted in the air. Silently a pair of binoculars was handed to her. She seized them and lifted them to her eyes.

'Don't look at the sun,' Angelos said sharply.

She found the eagles, though it was hard, as they started to soar upwards on thermals, to keep them in view. But it was an incredible sight to see. Reluctantly she handed back the binoculars. Angelos took them and refocused them for his eyes. Her gaze went from the eagles to him. He was completely absorbed. Completely, she realised with a little jolt, at home here on this high place.

She went on looking at him, her feelings strange.

After a while the eagles were out of sight, and Angelos let the binoculars drop. He turned back to Thea. For a moment she could not look away. Yet both their gazes were veiled by dark glasses.

I can see him, and he can see me, but we can't see each other...

The thought formed in her mind and seemed strange to her.

Abruptly he spoke, breaking the moment. 'How are your feet? Any blisters?'

She shook her head slowly. 'I don't think so. They're very good boots.'

'Yes, but you should have broken them in more easily. I set a hard pace on the way up.'

She didn't answer, just turned back to look at the panorama again, leaning forward, away from him.

Angelos looked at the back of her head. 'If it was too hard for you, you should have said.' He paused. 'I'd have slowed down.'

She still said nothing.

'You don't ask favours, do you, Kat?' he said slowly.

'I did once,' she said. Her voice was hollow. 'But I learnt my lesson.'

There was silence broken only by the keening wind.

'Not all of them,' said Angelos softly.

Her head turned and their eyes clashed unseeingly. Behind the safety net of her dark glasses she could only stare at him.

'What do you mean?' Her voice was sharp. He could hear a bite in it, but it was not of anger. Something different. Fear?

'Relax, Kat. Do you imagine I'm going to toss you over the edge?'

He saw her flinch, saw her try to stop it being visible. Emotion jabbed in him. He swore. Then, deliberately lightening the moment, he said, 'If nothing else, think of the scandal for me...'

'It could look like an accident. No witnesses.' Her voice was tight. Was she serious in what she said? She knew she wasn't—how could she possibly be?—and yet... 'It would be the ultimate destruction,' she heard her voice say.

He swore again volubly, in Greek. 'I should be angry with you for such an imputation! But I will make allowances for you. Kat.' He took a breath. 'You paid your dues. I made sure of that. So, whether you deny or admit your guilt for what you did, your slate is clean on that account. Now that you've relinquished the Honourable Giles I won't persecute you any further. But I couldn't let you make a fool of the man the way you made a fool of—'

He stopped. Then he climbed to his feet. 'Time to head back,' he said abruptly.

By the time they reached the chalet Thea was feeling it. Descending was harder on the muscles, she discovered, than ascending, and her legs were trembling by the time she was unlacing her boots in the chalet's porch. But she said nothing, made no complaint. Only nodded when Angelos, glancing at her, told her, 'Have a long soak in the bath before you do anything else.'

She did what he said, easing her aching muscles. Afterwards she wrapped herself up in the big fleecy bathrobe that came with the bathroom and padded out on to the balcony. It was early evening, no longer warm, and looking back along the valley she could see the lights of the village way below at the far distant end. Ahead of her, the huge open space was filled with darkening air, and high above pale stars were beginning to show in the sky, with the highest peaks still tinged with the last of the day's light.

She felt tired—tired in all her muscles—and yet

a sense of well-being held her. She didn't know why. It should be impossible. But it was so, all the same. For quite some time she stood there, arms resting on the wooden balcony, just looking out and feeling the improbable peace of the evening.

Everything seemed very far away. Very distant.

She tried to conjure Giles's face to mind, but it would not come. Only a handful of days ago she had thought her future lay with him, that she had achieved her heart's desire. But it had been ripped from her. Ripped to pieces.

Once before her life had been ripped to pieces. But she had remade it—better.

And I will do so again. As often as it takes.

She stared out over the darkening valley at the mountain peaks, high and pristine, untouchable. She didn't see the tall figure emerge at the far end of the balcony, his head turned towards her, standing as still as she, watching her.

Nor the questioning frown between his eyes as he did so.

Thea knew that dinner that night would not be easy, and when she went down, summoned by Trudi, the young maid, her tension levels were high again. She had dressed for comfort, wearing a pair of leggings and a long, soft sweater in teal-blue lambswool. She'd tied her hair up, and wore no make-up. Yet even dressed so casually she still felt Angelos's eyes on her as she walked into the lounge. He too was dressed casually, wearing another cashmere sweater—navy—with loose khaki chinos. He'd ruched back the sleeves of the sweater, and Thea moved her gaze away from his strong, tanned forearms. But looking at his face was no better. No better at all. His hair was damp, feathering at his nape and brow, and he was freshly shaved. She dragged her eyes away, looking instead at the wood fire crackling in the stone hearth. The whole room was ridiculously cosy, softly lit from old-fashioned lamps, with a huge rug in front of the hearth and sofas you could sink into.

Angelos was drinking a lager, and Franz, the older of the two manservants, dutifully asked what the *fraulein* might like to drink. Thea asked for fruit juice, and received a glass as tall as Angelos's, with similar pale gold contents, but the liquid was slightly fizzing apple juice.

'*Apfelsaft,*' Angelos enlightened. '*Sussmost*, as the Swiss call it. It's non-alcoholic.'

She sipped it cautiously and found it very re-freshing.

'How are your feet?'

'OK,' she said cautiously.

He nodded. 'Tomorrow we'll rest. You don't want to overdo it when you're inexperienced at mountain walking.'

She said nothing. What should she say? That she didn't want to be here in the first place? That she wanted to go home, to try and pick up what was left of her life now? Instead, she just followed Angelos through into the dining room—another comfortable room, with a large pine table, an-other open fire, and heavy dark green curtains on metal rings. There were thick candles on the table, already lit, although wall lamps gave the room light as well. She took the chair Franz held for her at the foot of the table, sitting down in the wide-based armed chair, padded with cushions. The whole effect was, she thought as she looked around, like a luxurious Alpine farmhouse. But it was warm and welcoming and homely. It was an odd description for a place owned by a man like Angelos Petrakos.

As Franz and the younger manservant, Johann, started to serve dinner, Thea realised, as she had

at lunch, that she was hungry. The food was hearty
and delicious. A rough pâté, followed by breaded
escalopes with fried potatoes and a root salad. It
was probably about a million calories, but right
now she didn't care. She tucked in.

Angelos watched her. 'It's the mountain air,' he
observed. 'It gives an appetite. And the exercise,
of course.'

She looked up.

'You're eating properly.' He explained his comment. 'I was beginning to wonder if you could.'

'You get used to chronic malnutrition as a
model,' she responded dryly.

'You really don't like the profession, do you?'
he returned, his voice even drier. Then his tone
changed. 'Was that one of Giles Brooke's attrac-
tions—he'd be taking you away from modelling?
Apart, of course, from his title and his money,' he
finished jibingly.

She was very still for a moment. Then she spoke.
'No.'

'Do you claim you were "in love" with him?'
The jibe was still there.

'No. But I cared for him, and I would have made
him the best wife I could.'

'Even though your marriage would have been based on a lie?'

She swallowed, looking away. She would not seek to placate him by saying she had accepted she had been wrong to deceive Giles. Why should she care what Angelos Petrakos thought of her? He was nothing to her—nothing! Except the man she hated…

From across the table Angelos's gaze rested on her. This evening she had made no effort to dress as she had in London and Geneva. Yet the casual attire did nothing to play down her beauty. The leggings highlighted the length of her legs, the long soft top skimmed her breasts and slender hips, the undressed hair, cinched at her nape, flowed down her back like a pale waterfall. Her face needed no make-up, no deepening of the eyes or reddening of the mouth. Her beauty was her own, whatever name she gave herself. Once again he felt the emotion he would not name flow through him.

She was so still…unmoving. She sat there making no reply, as if he had not spoken. Another emotion pricked within him—a familiar one. She was closing him out as if he had no effect on her. It angered him, as it had before. His fingers tightened on his knife and fork as he cut into his meat. He did not *want* her closing him out. He did not *want* her sitting there so still, as if he had no effect on her.

He knew better. She had stood there, motionless, while he had touched her, caressed her—kissed her. And he had known with every instinct, every certainty, that though she had come to him with nothing more than a venal motive she had, for all that, dissolved at his touch…

For a timeless moment it was vivid in his mind, that indelible memory. She had stood in front of him and he had explored the fineness of her skin, the contours of her face, tasted the softness of her mouth, silenced from its provocative insolence at last.

Memory—vivid, real—fused over his vision as his eyes rested on her now. He felt that unnamed emotion flow within him again. Compelling, ineluctable.

He picked up his glass, breaking the flow of that unnamed emotion. As he drank, he saw her start to eat again.

'So,' he began, setting down his glass, deliberately putting aside the thoughts that swirled inside his head, 'did you enjoy the walk this afternoon?'

Thea took a forkful of food. 'Yes.' She would be honest—why shouldn't she be if he wanted, for whatever inexplicable reason, to make polite conversation with her? But why he was doing so, why she was here at all, was beyond her comprehension. And certainly beyond her caring. She had no choice *but* to be here.

'You looked as though you did,' he said slowly. In his mind's eye he saw her again, sitting in the shelter of the rocks, gazing out over the vista, watching the eagles soaring. Quiet. Contemplative. Still.

As if she were at home there.

He put the thought aside, moved on from it.

'Next time we'll try a longer walk. But tomorrow you'd better take it easy. We'll drive down to the village and take the cable car up to the restaurant at the top of the ski slopes. It stays open for the summer season. There's a glacier nearby that makes summer skiing possible.

She looked up. 'I've never seen a glacier.'

There was a note of interest in her voice. Spontaneous, unguarded.

'They're an extraordinary phenomenon of nature,' said Angelos. 'Rivers of ice moving so slowly, but so powerfully. Though in geological time they are rushing rapids compared with the growth and erosion of the mountains. Yet the Alps themselves are striplings—one of the youngest mountain ranges in the world.'

Thea listened, realising that Angelos seemed to have a real interest in what he was telling her. He went on, explaining about tectonic plates, volcanic activity and mountain-building, and at a pause found herself saying, 'You know a great deal about it.'

His expression changed. 'I once wanted to be a geologist,' he said.

She stared. A geologist? Angelos Petrakos? Who could do anything he wanted?

'So why didn't you?'

'It wasn't possible,' he said flatly. 'Someone had to run the company my father had spent his life creating. It was my inheritance, and it was also my responsibility. I employ a lot of people whose livelihoods are in my hands. I can't jaunt off to do what I want. Only sometimes—like now—I come here, to the mountains. On my own.'

He frowned, as if he'd just realised what he'd said. Because he *wasn't* here on his own.

He didn't bring women here. It was a place he kept solely for his own use. The place he came when he could let go—briefly—the multiple complex threads of Petrakos International to be here on his own, among the mountains.

And no woman that he knew would want to be here. Those he chose for his liaisons would never have been content to spend their time in this deserted place—spend their days walking the ridges and peaks and cols all day. Nor could he envisage a single one of them discussing tectonic plates with him.

His frown deepened.

'Why have *you* an interest in geology?' he asked abruptly.

'Because I don't know anything about it,' she answered. 'There's still so much I don't know—about so many things.'

He was looking at her, with that unreadable expression in his eyes that she often saw there.

'"To be ignorant and uneducated is one thing,"' she said. '"To want to remain so is another."'

A glint showed in his eye. 'A noble expression,' he commented.

'It's what you said to me,' she answered, 'when I said I didn't know anything about Monte Carlo except that it was full of rich people.' She took a breath. 'I resented it at the time, but afterwards I remembered it.' She took a sip of her *appelsaft*. 'It was true—resent it as I did. Only fools stay ignorant by choice. So I chose to learn, instead.'

'You've learnt a great deal,' he said. 'You've changed almost beyond recognition. I don't just mean your appearance, your accent. Its much more than that.'

She looked away. 'You never knew me,' she replied.

'I knew enough.' His voice was harsh suddenly.

Involuntarily her eyes went back to him. Clashed with his. Then, abruptly, his eyes were veiled, and when he spoke again his voice was milder.

'And I still do.'

His voice was like silk across her skin.

Inside her ribs she could feel her heart give a sudden pulse. Danger pressed around her…

She felt it still, even after the meal had finished and they went into the lounge to have coffee served to them by Franz. As the manservant poured it out Angelos crossed to the well-stocked bookshelves behind the sofa in front of the hearth, and returned with a hefty atlas which he placed on the pine coffee table.

'You wanted to understand tectonic plates, and the formation of the Alps and other mountain ranges?' he said, settling himself down beside her and opening up the atlas.

Against her will, Thea found her interest out-weighing her resistance to having Angelos Petra-kos talk to her. Only as he used the illustrations and diagrams in the atlas to explain the compli-cated process she was disturbed by his physical proximity as he turned the pages. He was too close to her—far too close to her...

She felt her tension mount. Their bodies were almost within touching distance. As if he could feel it, he stopped talking, turning his head to hers. For an endless moment he looked at her.

Too close—too close! Far, far too close!

Her eyes flared in panic.

He straightened up, snapping the atlas shut. Without speaking he got to his feet and went across to an alcove. In a few moments music was flooding out into the room. It was Bach, or Viv-aldi, or something like that, she vaguely recog-nised. Bright and fast and corruscatingly brilliant. She was glad of it, and sat back into a corner of the sofa, drawing up her shoeless feet on to the seat, picking up her coffee cup, making a show of listening to the music.

She wondered whether Angelos was going to

start talking again, but he stayed silent, one long leg casually crooked across the other, occupying the rest of the sofa, seeming content to do as she was doing—drinking coffee and listening to the music. In the hearth, the pine logs crackled and spat, making the room warm, the atmosphere somnolent. The music slowed, and after a while Thea felt her eyelids grow heavy.

'You're falling asleep,' she heard Angelos say, and blinked. 'It's the fresh air and exertion. Go to bed, Kat.'

Slowly, sleepily, she uncoiled herself and set down the coffee cup, getting to her feet. For a moment she didn't quite know what to say. His expression was unreadable. Then she simply said, 'Goodnight,' and went to bed.

That night she slept even better, though her dreams were vivid of high, windy places and brilliant sun, and she dreamt she was still walking. When she awoke Trudi was hovering. Breakfast, so it seemed, was waiting for her, and the morning was advanced.

It was another bizarre day. After breakfast Angelos drove them down to the village and up to the cable car station. Soon they were suspended high above the now green ski slopes, traveling up to the restaurant poised beside the piste. They lunched out in the open on the decked surround, and once again Angelos proved an informative companion. Once again, Thea simply went along with it. What else could she do? All she could do was accept the situation—accept that it served his purpose for her to be here. Accept too, that— bizarre as it seemed—Angelos was treating her, as he had the previous day, without any sign of his habitual anger.

He took her to see the glacier after lunch—a short walk across the col—and pointed out its features, the sun dazzling on its ravined, icy surface. They talked of how the glaciers were shrinking in the Alps, and everywhere, and of global warming, and he told her how he had started a new division of Petrakos International to develop green technologies. Again she found her mind stimulated, her interest engaged, curiosity aroused. It helped, she knew, that in the bright sunlight dazzling off the glacier his dark glasses veiled his eyes from her, veiled hers from him. It seemed—safer.

The sun was already starting to dip behind the peaks opposite as they descended in the cable car again, and by the time they reached the village it was dusky and shadowed in the deep valley. But the little village was attractive, with summer window boxes and traditional wooden-framed shops and houses. She did some toiletries shopping, and then Angelos paused outside a *konditterei*.

'Tempted, Kat?' he murmured.

Thea gazed at the trays of exquisite chocolates. Then she shook her head. It was madness to think of eating such horrendously calorific sweetmeats. It took her a moment to realise Angelos had gone into the shop. He exited a few minutes later with a huge box, done up with an even huger bow. He presented the box to her with a flourish.

'For you,' he said.

And suddenly, out of nowhere, Thea felt her throat tighten. 'Th-thank you,' she heard herself say, taking the box.

Dear God, what was the world coming to? Angelos Petrakos buying her chocolates…

As if he did not hate her…

Immediately she repudiated the thought. Impossible—impossible to believe he did not hate her! Yet as the day turned into an evening spent as the one before, quietly over dinner and then in the lounge listening to music, that same strange *rapprochement* seemed to hold.

In the days that followed they settled down into what gradually became a familiar routine—heading off on one long Alpine walk after another, trekking in the dazzling sunshine across the close-cropped turf, along the steep, precipitous ridges. She could not but start to accept that, for a reason she could not fathom, it really *did* seem that Angelos had, inexplicably, dropped his long-held hostility towards her. He made no more jibes or challenges to her. Instead, as the days passed, he seemed to be treating her as if she were truly a guest—someone he'd chosen to spend time with. Someone whose life he had never destroyed.

It was the strangest realisation. And, whilst that was strange, she found her own response even stranger, even more inexplicable. Little by little, day by day, she started, in return, to find satisfaction in the long, strenuous walks that ranged far and wide over the slopes and ridges, to find stimulation in their talking over dinner, the time she spent with him. And with every passing day she realised, with confused disbelief, that in spite of everything that had passed between them she was beginning to feel, of all things, quite extraordinarily and totally against all expectations, a kind of rapport with him…finding herself content both

to trek in peaceful silence and to converse anima-
tedly, incisively, on any and every subject.

Yet even as her guard against him lowered, so
her physical awareness of him—which had always
disturbed and dismayed her—grew. Fervently she
tried to suppress it, tried to ignore it, but it was
there running like a silent, powerful river deep
inside her. She could not rid herself of it, could
not make herself insensible to it. It was there all
the time, growing. She knew her eyes were always
going to him—they were now, as they crossed a
col towards the next peak, on the taut planes of his
face, the strong features, the wind-ruffled sable
hair, the lean, powerful body. He was imprinting
himself more and more on her consciousness.

It was troubling and disturbing. And very, very
potent, bringing with it, slowly and inexorably,
the most troubling realisation of all.

She stopped dead in her tracks. Her mind
sheered away, like an eagle urgently beating its
wings to gain uplift against the plunging wind.

*No—that could not be—could not! It was im-
possible—impossible...*

Stumbling, she forced herself to move again,
missing her footing for a moment, so that she had

to exert all her balance to recover. To recover more than her footing…

Her eyes went to the man ahead of her, striding onwards.

And she felt her lungs hollow as if all the air around her had been sucked away, leaving nothing in its place but a truth she had to face. A truth that drained the blood from her face.

She didn't want to leave. Didn't want to go. Didn't want to go back to a world, a life, that seemed more and more unreal—more and more far away. Wanted only to go on being here, in this high, remote place.

With Angelos.

CHAPTER EIGHT

A CRESCENT moon was lying like a sliver of silver light, just above the dark mass of the mountains. Angelos stood on the balcony, hands curled over the balustrade, ignoring the chill of the night.

What was happening to him? For days now he'd taken Kat out across the mountains, walking for hours across the roof of the world, and with every passing day his thoughts about her had been changing. He knew it—could feel it. Could feel the emotions flowing through him like a watercourse finding a new path.

His brow furrowed frowningly. He had deliberately brought her here to these mountains, to this high, lonely place which exposed the truth about a person, giving them no place to hide, to disguise what they were. He knew that it was here that he became the person he most truly was— not the head of a huge multinational corporation, with thousands of employees and dozens to do his bidding at the nod of his head or his briefest word of instruction, but simply the man beneath that. The man he would have been had his father not worked his life away to build the company he'd bequeathed—too soon, far too soon—to his son. The burden along with the wealth and power. Here, in these mountains, he was himself.

And Kat—or Thea—or whatever name she called herself—was she the person she truly was here? Was that what he was seeing now? The truth exposed by the mountains that let no one hide their true selves here?

One thing he was certain of—his anger towards her had gone.

When it had happened he could not tell. But at some point the keening wind had whipped away the last shreds of it, like rags that had become tattered over the years and were now no more. It was strange not to feel angry with her any more. Strange to feel that now he could simply lay that long-carried emotion aside and allow himself to focus only on the woman who had become in this place, sharing this strange, unexpected affinity, his companion…

His unblinking gaze rested on the crescent moon. He let the word resonate in his mind. *Companion…*

Had any woman ever been a companion to him? His experience of women was wide, but he could think of none who would have wanted to come here. None he would have wanted here.

But the woman he had brought here, to find out the truth about her—that woman, and that woman only, he *did* want here. Whoever she had once been, whatever she had once done, seemed very distant to him now. Now the only reality he saw was a woman whose company seemed to fit his in every way, whether it was in the companionship of the shared trail, the long silences of their treks, the mutual appreciation of the stark beauty of the alpine landscape, or in the easy, unstilted conversation of their evenings on any and every subject their discourse led them to, or the quiet enjoyment of music and the fireside.

His hands tightened over the wooden railing. There was one other reality that he knew about her. About himself.

His weight shifted restlessly.

With every day spent with her that reality became clearer, stronger. With every day her extraordinary beauty haunted him more powerfully, drew him more ineluctably. And now, as he stood here, beneath the heavens, high above the world below, he knew with absolute certainty what he wanted above all. It no longer mattered how she had offered him her body five years ago. If she was truly the woman she seemed now to be, whom he no longer had to be angry with, then surely there was no reason why he should not, finally, consummate his long desire for her?

And hers for him. Because, for all her vehement protestation that night in London, when she had shrilled at him that she could not bear him to touch her, he knew—oh, he *knew*!—that she was lying. With every day, with every evening spent with her, he could feel like an electric charge her shimmering awareness of him. She could deny it all she liked—but for how much longer?

Day by day it brought him closer to her acceptance of what was between them. Day by day it brought him closer to the consummation he sought. It could not be long now…

And after?

For a moment he felt his mind hover over the question, circling like an eagle, then wheel away, leaving it unanswered.

Unanswerable…

He turned away, relinquishing his hold on the

railing, heading back indoors, downstairs. A new emotion filled him.

Anticipation.

Thea paused, knowing she had to step through the doorway into the dining room, just as she had every evening for the past week and more, but knowing that her reluctance now was quite, quite different from the reluctance she had felt that first evening here.

Completely different.

She was still shaken by the revelation that had swept over her that afternoon out on the mountainside. Still trying to reject the realisation that had forced itself upon her, yet knowing how hopeless it was to do so. Because, as she made herself go forward into the dining room, she could only feel the swirling, inchoate emotions circling within her. Could only feel the rushing in her lungs making her suddenly breathless as her eyes lighted on Angelos once again. His physical presence dominated her senses, made her feel shaky, overwhelmed her.

Did he see her reaction? For a brief instant she thought she saw his eyes flicker, but then it was gone, and he was—as he always was these days—

his usual self, greeting her briefly, waiting to take his seat while Franz pulled out her chair for her.

To counter the emotions swirling within her she made a play of shaking out her napkin, settling herself, smiling at Franz as he said something to her which she didn't quite catch. She nodded her head politely and poured herself a glass of water, trying to keep her hands steady, to breathe evenly despite the raggedness of her breath, the rapid pulse in her veins. Her eyes lifted to the figure at the head of the table.

And immediately she knew that what she had discovered about herself was true—hopelessly, helplessly true. That if, right now, she could walk out of here and never set eyes on Angelos Petrakos ever again—she would not go. She would stay here, her breath caught in her lungs, and go on gazing at him, just gazing, while emotions chased each other round her body—gazing at him, at the turn of his head as he talked to Franz, at his strong, tanned features, so familiar now, so—

'Gnadige, fraulein—'

The voice at her side made her drag her hapless gaze away, and she blinked. As Franz was being detained by Angelos, it was Johann who was holding out a bottle for her view, with an enquiring

expression on his face. She could see the word
'*apfel*' on the bottle, and nodded abstractedly.
Then her eyes were sucked back to Angelos.

Her heart-rate quickened.

He nodded with finality to Franz, and the man
moved away. As Angelos turned his attention
back to her. Immediately, urgently, she dropped
her gaze. For something to cover her shaken state,
she reached for the newly filled glass at her side.
She took a long draft, for her mouth was suddenly
dry. Briefly it registered that the apple juice tasted
different from the way it usually did, but she had
no mental capacity to pay it any regard—all the
focus of her mind was on controlling her reaction
to Angelos Petrakos.

Because control it she must. That was essential. Essential not to let that fluttering deep inside
her—as if a bird were beating its wings somewhere—take her over. Essential not to let her eyes
hang on him, drinking in his face, his features,
the very being of him. Essential to make it appear,
at least, even if it were a hopeless lie, that all she
felt about him was what she had always felt.

She dipped her gaze, though it was an effort,
and smiled at Franz as he placed their first course
in front of her. Absently she took another mouth-

ful of apple juice to give herself something to do. The taste was less different this time, and it seemed to quench her thirst more—be slightly less sweet. She drank again, more deeply, feeling the juice warming through her, quickening her senses, it seemed to her. Then she picked up her knife and fork and made great concentration on the artfully folded arrangement of cold meats, furrowing her brow as she did so.

All the time she was burningly conscious, more than ever before, of Angelos Petrakos at the far end of the table.

She had always been aware of him—always! The impact he made on her senses had always been overpowering. But it had always been countered by the long, bitter resentment of him that had filled her for so many years with fierce, implacable hatred.

But now—

I don't hate him any more.

The words formed in her head and hung there, suspended, as she felt her mind enfold them.

No more hatred...

How it had happened, she did not know. It had been in the days spent here, the time spent with him, seeing him anew, as if the harsh, punishing, pitiless being she had once known was no longer there and she no longer had to hate him.

It was as if a burden were slipping from her. A burden she had carried so long, so unrelentingly. And as it slipped from her shoulders she felt a sense of release go through her. A lightening of her whole being. As if she were finally, finally free.

Free to feel, finally, what she was filled with now. Free to do, finally, what she was doing now—letting her eyes gaze upon him freely, openly, taking in everything about him, wanting to do nothing else but hold this moment...

How she got through the meal, Thea did not know. Time seemed to be doing something strange, for it seemed to take both a huge length of time and be over in a flash. What they talked about she had no idea. Her mind seemed to be losing focus, and yet everything about him seemed to be in super-focus, dominating her consciousness. She seemed to be feeling strangely relaxed, which was odd, because she knew that her awareness of Angelos's intense physical presence had never been greater. She could see him, it seemed, in absolute detail.

She kept noticing things impinge on her consciousness—tiny, inconsequential things, but they caught her attention, made her see them, become aware of them, permeating her mind like a running commentary...

He's shaved. His jawline's quite smooth. His hair is still slightly damp, feathering at his nape. His brow, his eyes are flecked, his lashes thick. The lines around his mouth were incised. His wrists are lean, his hands square, powerful. But the fingers are long, and the way they hold his fork, his wineglass, makes me want to watch, to look...

So she did—just looked. Gazed.

He didn't seem to mind that she was not responding very intelligently to his conversation, even though she was aware that her comments seemed disjointed, abstracted. Every now and then she saw a flicker of his eyes, and it intrigued her. She wanted to watch for it. It came again, and she felt, deep in her body, an answering flicker.

'Shall we go next door?'

She blinked, his dark, deep voice catching her unawares. She glanced at the table and realised that dinner was over. She got to her feet and for the briefest moment felt very dizzy. Then the feeling passed and she shook her head slightly. She saw there was still some apple juice left in her glass—Johann had refilled it, she recalled, during dinner—and drained it to clear her head. There would be coffee next door, set out, as always, by the staff, who then went off duty for the remainder of the evening, retiring to their quarters in the spacious chalet.

In the lounge she curled up, as she always did, at one end of the deep sofa, Angelos at the far end. But this night the cushions seemed softer, it seemed, her limbs more relaxed, the warmth of the fire more embracing. Everything seemed softer, slower, with a kind of glow about it all. A sense of well-being pervaded her, of being enclosed and safe, the outer world so far away, nothing more than a dream. Only here was real, only now was real, and everything was at once both bathed in a strange soft focus, and incredibly, wondrously vivid. It was a feeling she had never had before.

She reached forward to pour the coffee. The pot seemed heavier than usual, the flow of liquid slower, and her wrist dipped slightly as she handed his cup to him. He set it down on his end of the coffee table with a murmur of thanks, then poured himself his customary cognac, leaning back to swirl it slowly, contemplatively, in its balloon glass. She found herself watching it, eyes drawn to its slow swirl as he lifted the glass to his nose, but did not drink. She found herself wondering why.

The fire was burning low, and he got to his feet, kneeling down beside the hearth to add more logs. Thea's eyes followed him. He was wearing one of his cashmere sweaters, and she had a sudden yearning to feel the extreme softness of the wool under her hand. She watched him cross to the alcove which contained the ferociously high-tech music equipment, and while she watched, thinking again how tall and lithe his powerful frame was, her eyes caught the cognac glass perched on the table. Strangely curious, she reached to pick it up, holding it as he did, swirling the contents slowly. Then she dipped her nose to catch the fragrance.

It was heady stuff! She inhaled again, feeling a strange light-headedness, and inhaled once more, even more deeply. It was an extraordinary scent—complex and evocative. She inhaled again, face over the glass, experiencing again that buoyant light-headedness that seemed so very pleasant. Then, as Angelos returned to his seat, she hastily put the glass back, her attention diverted by the music now filling the room.

Her eyes lit, pleasure filling her—Rachmaninov, his variations on a theme of Paganini, lush and poignant, pouring out over her, making her heart lift with emotion. The music swelled in its ecstatic melody, sweepingly beautiful. As the crescendo came, and the main theme soared, her breath caught, lips parted. She was filled with emotion—powerful and uplifting. Her eyes went instinctively, irresistibly, to Angelos.

He met her gaze full-on, dark eyes holding hers, and she was completely incapable—of breaking away from his. She saw them flare, a sudden blaze in them, and emotion seized her, overwhelming her. She could not break her gaze, could only let him hold it as effortlessly as the orchestra held the sweeping melody. She listened, rapt, enraptured. Filled with an emotion that swelled within her even as the music swelled.

At length the music ended—but not the emotion filling her… That wonderful, heady, swirling emotion was still possessing her…

What was happening to her? To feel so intensely, so vividly as she did now! So incredibly moved…

She did not know, could not tell—knew only

that the whole of her being was focused here, now, on this moment. This time. This space.

This man.

The music changed. Slow violins, delicate— quite different from the impassioned strains of Rachmaninov. But they were just as evocative in their own unearthly way, weaving, so it seemed to her, a net of sound, diffusing into the air. She felt alive, vivid, as she had never felt before.

A sound made her turn her head. A log had fallen in the fire, opening up its glowing heart. She watched as Angelos set down his cognac once more and crossed to hunker down on the pale soft rug, reaching for more wood to rebuild the fire.

On impulse—she did not know why, only that she wanted to, right now, while in this strange, breathless mood—she slid on to the floor, kneeling by the table, stretching her hand out not for her undrunk coffee but for his cognac glass. She wanted to inhale its bouquet again, wanted to feel that pleasurable light-headedness that had come last time. She lifted it to her mouth, letting her lip curve over the glass edge to sample the fragrance within. It was less powerful now, and she tilted the glass more. The cognac touched her lips, and without her volition she realised she was opening

her mouth to it. It filled her mouth with liquid
fire, and for a moment she almost gasped. Then
it had slipped down her throat, leaving a burning wake. Her eyes widened, and she felt the fire
snake down. Blinking, she set the glass back and
picked up her coffee cup, draining it rapidly to
quench the fire.

She'd been foolish, she knew, to do what she
just had—and yet, amazingly, right now she didn't
care. Didn't care because inside her a warmth
was spreading—a warmth that seemed to wash
through her, through every cell of her body.
Taking her over. Her vision seemed to blur for
a moment, then cleared—with a clarity she had
never known before. Behind her, very close, Angelos was tending the fire, hunched down on the
soft, large sheepskin rug that stretched between
the sofa and the hearth, brushing his hands free of
wood dust. His cashmere sweater stretched over
the sculpted musculature of his back. She could
see the softness of the fabric, moulding his lean,
hard body. Could see, with a strange, luminous
clarity, her hand reaching out, the tips of her fingers brushing, scarcely touching, the fine, soft
wool.

He stilled, hands pausing in their movement,

then hunkered back, twisting as he did so. She drew back her hand. He didn't speak, only shifted so that he was, she vaguely recognised, now sitting on the rug, one knee drawn up, the other splayed. He crooked his arm around his knee and reached for his cognac. Vaguely, she felt she should get back on to the sofa, but it was comfortable here, leaning back against it. She watched him take a mouthful of his cognac, his eyes holding hers.

They were so dark—a deep, drowning dark— and she gazed into them. Everything was very clear, like crystal, and yet only *he* was in focus. It was strange…so strange. She went on gazing at him. In the background the music crept, slow and somnolent, weaving its net about her senses. Behind him, the fire crackled softly, its warm light glowing. The lights in the room, too, seemed softer, shadows pooling.

He sat, arm crooked, the slow, rhythmic swirling of his glass flickering in her vision, but she could not look away from him. She could feel, somewhere, that her heart had started to beat—as if till now it had never done so. But now the pulse was tangible, like a low, aching throb.

She wanted to reach out—wanted to let the tips of her fingers brush down again lightly, so lightly, on the soft, luxurious surface of the cashmere. She could feel her hand lift, and as it did, his voice stayed her.

'Wait.'

His voice came low and deep, with an imperative note in it. Her eyes gazed into his questioningly, confused. He spoke again, in that same low, intense voice.

'I must know—is this truly what you want?'

His eyes were playing over her face, searching. Searching for the answer he sought—wanted so much. Had waited for so long, it seemed. All evening he had felt the power of his response to her released, accepted finally, and now, in this intimate setting, he was on the point of achieving what he knew he wanted with every part of his being. Her beauty was intoxicating, haunting—his desire for her was consuming. But after all that had been between them, all the anger and strife and bitterness, it had to be right—right for her. He had made his peace with her—was this now, finally, her making peace with him?

His eyes searched hers, needing an answer.

For one long moment she simply gazed with limpid clarity, revealing everything she felt about him at that moment, everything she wanted. Then she spoke one word only. A breath, a sigh…

'Yes…'

She could see the sudden blaze in his eyes, hear the catch of breath in his throat. Feel in her veins her own pulse beat. The air was thick. Thick, the blood in her veins. The emotion she could not name, could only feel with a shimmering intensity all through her body, was creaming through her. All she wanted was here, now…this moment.

This man…

And slowly, very slowly, her eyes still clinging to his, she did what she wanted. Reached out with the tips of her fingers to brush the rich softness of his cashmere sleeve. He sat completely still, not even swirling his depleted cognac, just holding her eyes as her fingers brushed the soft fabric. Then her fingers reached further, rounding over the contours so that her palm was curved around his sleeve. Beneath the fabric she could feel the muscled sinew of his arm. Hard against the softness of the wool. Her hand curled over it, feeling the warmth of his body seeping through into her palm.

Then slowly, very slowly, she lifted her hand away.

For a long, long moment she could only sit, legs

slanted away from him, meeting his gaze. Around her the music wove its web and the soft firelight played on the strong features of his face, flickering in the shadows of the room.

She heard him murmur something honeyed and mellifluous. Then his hand was reaching forward. The other still cupped his cognac glass, but the outstretched one was turning, so that the back of his hand was brushing slowly, so slowly, down the sleeve of her top.

She could not move, could not breathe, could only twine her eyes with his while the back of his hand stroked down her arm. Lightly. Then it lifted again. This time to her cheek.

It was light, so light, his touch. Almost not there. And yet her breath stilled in her lungs. His long, strong fingers were cupping her chin, tilting it upwards, and then his long lashes swept down over his eyes and his head was lowering.

The brush of his lips on hers was like snow drifting, as light as snowflakes melting on her lips.

He brushed them softly, so softly, and her eyelids fluttered closed, to feel the bliss of it. Because bliss it was. Bliss to have that soft, sensuous touch of his mouth on hers. He murmured something, but she did not know what it was. Then both hands were cupping her face, lifting it to him, and his mouth was opening hers...

Soft and warm and blissful—so, so blissful.

He was drawing her down, his arms coming around her to ease her across his body, cradling her as his mouth moved on hers. Pleasure filled her. Sweet, sensuous pleasure. Firing through every nerve ending, drawing her down, down, down into its seductive depths.

She was lying beside him on the warm, soft, fleecy rug, the fire hot on her back. He was kissing her still, murmuring to her, and his arms were cradling her, his hand running softly, so softly, along her spine. She was wordless and speechless and could only lie there being kissed so softly, so sensuously, so blissfully.

Whatever else existed in the world was no longer there. There was only this—this warm, velvet sensation at her mouth, his hand at her nape, sliding the restraining fastening from her hair so that it fell in a long, pale wave across the rug. He murmured again—words she could not hear but only feel, like a fine vibration through her whole body. His fingers, long, and sensitive, threaded through her hair, and the sensation on her scalp was a soft, evocative tingling. The wonderful headiness in her mind consumed her. She felt the sensual delight of his mouth moving against hers, his body strong and lean, and her hands curled over his shoulders, kneading into the aching softness of the cashmere to meet the sinewed resistance of his flesh. She wanted to feel that smoothness, that muscle and sinew, and she moved restlessly in his arms. Her hands slid down his torso to his waist, and her questing fingers found the space beneath the soft wool. Oh, it was bliss—*bliss* to run her hands along the hard, smooth contours, warm to her touch, to let her arms wind around him, palms splaying out across his spine, the sculpted perfection of his back.

His kiss deepened, and now she was lying on her back. She did not know how, knew only that her hands were being taken and lifted over her head. He was arched over her, his mouth still moving on hers, but now his lips lifted away and he was gazing down at her as she lay beneath him, his hands holding hers. Her narrow skirt had twisted around her limbs, so that she could not move them, but she did not want to. She wanted only to lie here in the warmth, with the strange, overpowering headiness in her senses. She lay still, gazing up at him. His eyes bored into hers, and she gazed upwards into pools of night.

His hand was at her waist, gliding upwards beneath her top, skimming, so lightly, the surface of her skin beneath her breasts. Her breath caught again, and then he was easing the material upwards, lifting it over her head, peeling it off, casting it aside. And then, his task done, his gaze returned to her.

She lay, hands caught in his, hair streaming loose over the fleece of the rug, bared to his view, his touch.

Arched above her, Angelos gazed his fill.

She was his.

Now—this night, this moment—now. The waiting was over—fulfilment was *now*. Emotion surged in him—desire flowing like an unstoppable tide as she lay beneath him, her body his at last. So incredibly, extraordinarily beautiful—the extreme slenderness of her torso, the incredible grace of her shoulders, her arms, and the high, rounded, exquisite breasts.

Past and present merged. But this time he did not have to deny himself—did not have to put her away from him, thrust her from him with harsh, contemptuous words. No need for that now. And

from her there was no more hatred, no more wariness, no more hostility. No more defences.

Only the warm, soft ardour of her body, the
longing in her eyes, her touch.

This time she was his, completely.

His hands lifted to her breasts, shaping them
with the tips of his fingers, while the unnamed
emotion creamed within him. The coral tips hardened at his touch, and she gave a low, helpless
sound in her throat that sent the blood surging in
his body. Her eyes were glazed, unfocussed now,
and her aroused lips were softly parted.

The languor of desire was upon her.

Waiting for his possession.

Slowly he lowered his head once more. But not
to taste her lips. As his mouth grazed the straining peak of her breast he heard that low noise in
her throat again. Arousal quickened in him.

And in her.

He could feel it—feel the sudden tensing in her
body, feel her wrists pulling against his as her
body tautened like a bow. He suckled her again,
more strongly, and felt again that torsion in her
spine, the low moan in her throat. He moved his
mouth, trailing across the satin skin to the slight
valley between her exquisite breasts, allowing

himself for a little while no more than the pleasure of her flawless bloom, before reaching for her other peak, laving and arousing it, until he could feel her move restlessly, wrists flexing against his hand.

And then suddenly he could wait no longer. He had waited so long for her, but no longer. In a movement as swift as it was sudden he scooped her up, lifting her slight weight into his arms as he got to his feet. Her eyes flared, but he was already striding from the room, sweeping her up the stairs, her bared torso crushed against him, her head on his shoulder and her hair like a banner streaming over his arm.

Beautiful—so incredibly beautiful...

Emotion surged in him again, and his arms tightened around her. He took her to his room, pulling back the feather duvet and lowering her down. Then, with ruthless control of his own impulses, he stripped the clothes from his body, impatient, urgent.

Then he was there with her again. More words came from him—he knew not what—knew only that as she lay there, the dark swathe of her skirt twisted around her limbs, her pale, high breasts still peaked, aroused, the extraordinary beauty

of her face still transfigured, that his arousal was
so intense he must exert every strenuous effort to
control his own desire for her.

But it was hard, excruciatingly hard, to do so!
With punishing slowness he eased her skirt from
her, and as his eyes went to her his breath caught.
Her breasts alone had inflamed him, but to see
her slender, naked body, all for him, was beyond
pleasure. Beyond anything he had ever known.

Slowly, sensually, his hands smoothed down her
silken body.

She was mindless, hazed with arousal, her body
a mesh of sensation—sensation such as she had
never known before. Her breasts strained, their
peaks aching with desire. But his hands had
left them, gliding down her flanks sensuously,
sinuously, flaring over the line of her hips. At
the vee of her thighs, his thumbs met. Slowly,
watching her all the time as she gazed blindly up
at him, as the world swirled slowly around her in
sinuous whorls of pleasure, she felt the pressure
of his thumbs indent, bear down.

Instinctively, she parted for him. A need as old
as time. An ache as deep as her core. She was
melting, she could feel it, liquefying as the soft,
glistening folds of her flesh parted for his explor-

ing, sensual caress. It was like being taken into another world! How could there be such sensation? How could anything feel so blissful, so beautiful, so exquisitely pleasurable? And the pleasure was increasing—building remorselessly, like fire licking through her veins, inflaming her, possessing her.

She moved against him. She could not stop herself. Again it was instinctive, insistent. Her hips lifted to him, her head moving restlessly on the pillow of her hair, her hands lifting to close over the cusps of his bare shoulders, to tighten. He was murmuring to her, but she could not hear, could only feel—her whole body was nothing but sensation, a pool of living fire, consuming itself as the exquisite caresses aroused her so that the heat fanned her skin, dissolved through her flesh, became one with it. Each touch was bliss—bliss upon bliss. Deeper, more arousing, reaching into her core, so that the muscles of her thighs strained, hips lifting, wanting more…more…

Then there was yet more sensation—and she rippled with the pleasure of it, gasped at her sensitivity to it. Her breathing was shallow, urgent—her lips parted, neck arching back. The fire licking in her veins was melting her, dissolving her, flush-

ing through her like an unstoppable tide—a wave
that was building, building. And she wanted more,
more—it was unbearable, unbearable…

And then it broke—broke in a wave of sensation so intense, so absolute, that she cried out.
She could not stop herself—could only ride out
on the wave to the uttermost ends of the universe
as her body buckled and convulsed, with wave
after wave, scorching and searing. She was blind,
deaf—insensible to anything, everything, that
was not this incredible, unstoppable tide that was
going on, and on, and on…

Angelos stilled, his whole focus on the visible
expression of the orgasm flashing through her
body. Her head was threshing, hips straining, her
eyes blind, and across her breasts and belly the
flush of desire consuming itself flared hotly. His
stillness lasted a few seconds only. Then, with
an urgency that was unstoppable, he reached for
a silvered packet. Moments later he was ready
for her. Ready to take the same pleasure he had
given her—would give her now again. Arching
over her, he gazed down once more. Her beauty
inflamed him. The intensity of her response to
him was like a light within her glowing body. She
was possessed by desire.

And now to be possessed by him.

Slowly, exquisitely, he eased into her.

She was tight—tight like a sheath made for a sword—and for a moment he had to still, for his arousal was so intensified by the pressure that he had to pause. She, too, he realised dimly, had stilled as well, her hands folded over the cusps of his shoulders, fingers suddenly indenting into his skin. A noise had come from her—inarticulate, like a gasp, a cry. It seemed to trigger him, and he moved deeper within her.

Oh, but she was tight! A thought flashed in his mind—absurd, impossible. He thrust it from him as sensation overpowered him. She was sheathing him so tightly that it was an exquisite torment to be so full within her. And yet he must ensure her pleasure, too. He gazed down at her. Her eyes were shut, the intensity of the expression on her face as if the world had stopped for her. At his shoulders he could feel the pads of her fingers, her nails pressing deep into him. As if she, too, were under the same exquisite control that he was exerting on himself.

Well, he would release that control—release it in her—and then finally, finally, in him.

Every muscle in his back straining, he began to move.

He watched her expression change. Her eyes still did not open, and he knew their focus would be inward, extracting every last gram of sensation from his possession of her. Just as he was doing. His movements were minute, under his absolute control. He could feel sweat beading along his spine with the effort it took to control his own reaction, his own overwhelming urge to plunge deep within her to reap his own satiation.

But she must find hers first. Her body was still in that state of absolute arousal he had engendered, and now he must take it that final step. He moved again, feeling her tightness flex around him, hearing once again that high, unearthly sound in her throat. He was on the edge, on the blade of a knife, as he moved to intensify the pressure not of her tightening around him, but of him against that most sensitive place within her, where the mesh of nerve endings created the physical locus of consummation. The high, helpless gasp came again, and he could feel, as if in slow motion, each nail indenting into his flesh. Feel simultaneously the slight but fatal tilting of her pelvis, sending him hurtling over the edge of the knife blade.

He surged within her, and in the sheeting sensation that engulfed him he realised that it had happened to her as well. That cry was coming from her again, with unbearable intensity, and he surged again, peaking within her in hot, unstoppable satiation, feeling as he did so the threshing convulsion of her muscles enclosing him, drawing him into her more tightly yet as he swept her body against his, feeling her convulsing and trembling within his clasp.

It went on and on, the incredible, unstoppable release, with an intensity of sensation that drenched through him. Had he ever, *ever* felt this way before at such a moment? Ever felt this extremity of satiation?

Then, after an eternity of sensation, it was ebbing from him, draining him of all his strength. He folded down, still with her body in his arms, taking her with him. She was ebbing, too—he could feel it. Her body was still giving little tremors in his arms, and the soft little cries in her throat made him clasp her more tightly yet.

His hand was stroking her hair, soothing her. He was murmuring to her—words he hardly understood himself, hardly heard beneath the tumult of his heartbeat. She lay in his arms, so still, her satin skin dewed with moisture. He could feel the pulsing beat of her heart, so close to his...

His voice, when he spoke, was low and resonant.

'I have the final truth about you now—no more denial. You said you could not bear me to touch you! But this...*this*...' his mouth lowered to hers one last, lingering time '...this tells me the truth. At last...'

His kiss was slow, and sealing, and then, his eyelids heavy with the aftermath of desire fulfilled, he felt his vision dim, his heart-rate slow, and with her warm and folded in his arms he gave himself to sleep.

CHAPTER NINE

ANGELOS stirred drowsily. Something was wrong.

He was alone.

Instantly his eyes sprang open.

She had gone.

In one lithe, fluid movement he had jack-knifed up out of the bed, eyes casting around in the dawn light that was reaching the edges of the curtained windows, then was striding into the *en suite* bathroom.

Not there.

He frowned. Had she gone back to her room? Ripping a towel from the rail, he wrapped it cursorily around his hips, went out on to the landing, opened her bedroom door. The bed was unused, unslept in. Her *en suite* bathroom empty.

Where the hell was she?

Emotion spiked in him. He didn't know what it was, and he wasn't in any kind of mood to be introspective. He was only in the mood to find her.

Without thinking, he slid back the glass doors

to the balcony, but there was no sign of her there, either, in the chill early morning. Frustration bit in him—and incomprehension. He thrust back from the balustrade to head indoors, his gaze unconsciously sweeping out across the precipitous slope beyond. But even as it did so his muscles froze. His whole body froze.

There, on the descending slope far to the left of the chalet, where the curve of the road indented, he saw a lone figure, heading down the side of the mountain. Walking rapidly, haltingly, hurriedly.

For an endless moment time stopped. Then, disbelievingly, he realised who it was.

He wheeled around, heading back into his own room, yanking open the doors further along the balcony, knowing he had to get dressed with the least possible delay. But even as he threw open the doors of his closet his eyes went to his empty bed, the quilt thrown back.

And time stopped again. His gaze froze as he stared at the exposed sheet.

Disbelief knifed through him.

And much, much more.

Within minutes he was dressed, booted, kitted up—and in pursuit.

* * *

Thea was walking. Walking as fast, as urgently as she could. Her head was throbbing, her heart was pounding, skin clammy. She felt sick and cold—so cold—despite the windproof jacket. She had to make the road—make it as fast, as speedily as she could down the unfamiliar track that was a much more direct route to the road below than the hairpin track up to the chalet. But it was a treacherous path, she discovered. Hardly there in places, narrow and precipitous. Her leg muscles were cold, resistant after the previous day's long trek, and her legs were not all that ached.

Between her thighs aching pain made each step a torment.

But it was a pain she welcomed. *Punishment.* Punishment for what she had done.

No! She must not think of that. Time enough to think of that—dear God, time enough! Now, all her strength must be on what she was doing now.

Escaping.

Her legs were trembling, there was dull, raw ache in her pelvis, sick muzziness in her head and clawing at her stomach, sick breathlessness in her lungs. Desperately, she hurried on. Sometimes her footing on the dew-drenched grass slipped, scaring her, but she recovered and pressed on. Always.

The light was growing brighter all the time, the sun fingering over the far mountain. Day was here, and time was running out. She quickened her pace, half stumbling.

She dared not look back.

The path was getting steeper, the slope convex now, so she could not see the road below any more. But it must be there, and she must press on—press on. She was desperate for water, but had brought none with her, not daring to waste time filling a water bottle. Her mouth was parched, and the throbbing in her head had worsened. Acid was pooling in her stomach. Her gullet felt raw and scraped, her breath knifing through her lungs.

How long she walked she did not know—only knew that her thoughts were an agony. An agony of loathing.

For Angelos Petrakos.

For herself.

How—how had it happened? The question seared like a brand in her head. How had she let it happen? Memory stabbed like knives piercing her, twisting in her stomach.

I let him do it to me—I let him do it to me five years ago—just stood there while he touched me, kissed me, caressed me...then called me a whore...a whore...

Her throat clenched with pain. With shame. How could she have forgotten what he had done to her? How could she have let herself be lulled as she had, day by day, her guard against him lowering? Not seeing his intention, not understanding the danger she was placing herself in.

Until it was far, far too late.

Like an icy shower, she felt again that moment when she had faced the realisation that, impossible though it seemed, she had known that she didn't want to leave.

Oh, God, how could I have been so stupid—so unbelievably stupid?

She stared unseeing out over the lightening valley. To have come to such a pass...

I didn't want to leave him...

The words hollowed out inside her, each one a blow.

My fault—my fault—my fault.

Her fault, and hers alone—her stupidity, her folly.

Couldn't you see? Couldn't you see what he was doing?

But she hadn't—that was the agonising flagellating fact of it! She hadn't seen. She had been so beguiled, so self-indulgently overwhelmed by her own responsiveness to him, her electric awareness of him, that she hadn't realized. Fool, fool, *fool* that she was! Hadn't realised how he was using that for his own ends! Using her to fulfil the purpose he had brought her here for!

She heard his voice—the last words he'd spoken to her—tolling like doom in her head.

'I have the final truth about you now...'

The truth, terrifying and full of anguish, blazed in all its horror for her. That was why he had brought her here! Lulled her day after day into thinking his relentless hostility to her had ebbed, lured her into lowering her guard, making her so fatally, fatally weak...

So he could throw that in her face—mock her in his triumph over her!

Oh, God, to give myself to him like that—to offer myself on a plate! When all along...

She felt the sickness roil in her stomach again, the ache between her legs marking her shame— the stamp of his triumph over her, encompassing her destruction...

For a moment so brief she knew it was not real another memory cut across her torment.

Her body clinging to his. That wonder and amazement—that ecstasy that she had never dreamt of! It had made a living flame of her body, transporting her to a world, a universe she had never known existed. His arms around her, embracing her, wrapping her to him, folding her to him, holding her, while she cried out in wonder and bliss.

No! She wiped the memory from her mind. That was an illusion—nothing more than that! An illusion he'd wanted her to believe, for how else would he have got his triumph? Proving beyond doubt, beyond all her defiant denial, that she was exactly what he had accused her of being five long bitter years ago! And now all she could do was flee. Flee as fast, as far as she could.

She had survived him before. She would survive him now. She must.

The final knife turned in her, its blade reaching deepest of all. She was going to pay a price she had never known existed. That could never be expunged.

Never.

Bleakly, blindly, she blundered on, desperation in every stumbling step.

She had nearly crested the slope that bulged

from the main descent of the mountainside to the road still far below. The pathway was petering out, and she could only tread in what she hoped and prayed was the right direction. She scanned the way ahead, urgency pressing at her. The light was stronger now, sunshine blazing on the upper slopes above the chalet. She dared not look back to see how far she was, knowing how exposed she must be. She had to go on, as fast as possible...

And then, freezing the blood in her veins, she heard a shout behind her.

Like a hunted deer she halted, turned, and terror froze her. It was Angelos, coming down the path towards her. He was still a hundred metres or so above her, but his long stride swallowed up the path, zigzagging down to where she was. Panic seized her. She plunged on, slipping as she did so, grabbing at the grass to steady herself. She heard him shout again, but she only scrambled onwards, heart pounding sickly.

Then, as she looked ahead further at the path, she gave a smothered cry of dismay. Till now the convex slope had concealed what lay ahead. Now, as she finally cleared the curving angle, she saw that the path stopped abruptly, terminating where a sheet of rock and scree dropped sharply away. A landslip had sliced through the rest of the slope, taking the path with it. For a moment she just stood there, swaying. Then, over her head, she heard Angelos's voice.

'Kat—stay where you are! Don't move!'

Her head whipped round. He was only fifty metres above her now, cutting down vertically over the grass. Closing fast. She scrambled onwards, to where the path ended and the sheer rock face started. She heard him call again. Felt panic knife again.

She couldn't stop! She *couldn't*!

Urgency, desperation, drove her onwards. With a ragged breath she dropped to her knees and started to inch out across the bare, steep rock, using her hands and her feet together over the sheer surface. It was wet with condensation from the night air, slippery beneath her fingers and icy cold. Close up, its smoothness was deceptive, with jagged flakes and shallow shelves of scree increasing in the direction she was trying to traverse, across and down. It was madness to attempt it—there was scarcely a foothold or a handhold that she could use properly, and grabbing at one such only resulted in the heel of her hand being cut.

She whimpered in pain. Simultaneously her foot slipped, and her crouching position slid out into an open sprawl across the treacherous surface. She froze, spread-eagled, her toes in agony trying to keep her from sliding further down. She could see blood from her hand seeping on to the rock. The pain made her hand slip, and with the loss of hold she felt her body judder down the rockface further, her feet only encountering scrabbling scree that would not hold her. Desperately she clung on, shoulder sockets in agony, trying to force herself to make her next move. But fear paralysed her. And weakness. She had no strength left—none.

'Kat!'

The voice was right above her now, and she strained her face upwards. Angelos was on the grass ridge above the rock face, lying face-down, half hanging over. His hand was extended down towards her.

'Get my hand!' He strained it further forward—the maximum he could reach without falling himself.

He was nearly touching her. She gazed, blind with panic and dread.

'Lunge for my hand—I'll catch you. It's OK, I can pull you back up. Just do it, Kat—*do it*!'

He sounded so angry. Furious. His face was dark.

She saw him. Saw him clear, vivid.

Angelos Petrakos. The man who had destroyed her once, five long years ago. Who had taken Giles from her, destroyed all her hopes of that future. And who had now completed her destruction. Her utter destruction.

A destruction from which there could be no return...

'Kat—*take my hand*!'

She gazed up at him. Holding out his hand to her.

As if—dear God—Angelos Petrakos were trying to save her...

She wanted to laugh. Laugh with savage self-mockery at the idea that he might be trying to save her. But her lungs were frozen—her body could not laugh.

It could only convulse.

Loosening her frail, exhausted grip.

'*Kat!*'

It was the last sound she heard before her head hit against the rockface as she slid joltingly, vertically down and she lost consciousness. In her last moment of awareness something struck her as odd. Angelos hadn't sounded angry any more…

For a timeless moment Angelos was paralysed, watching Kat's helpless body jolting downwards, as if she were nothing more than a rag doll. Then, eventually, it reached a ledge and stopped.

There were voices. Thea could hear them. Dimly, as if from a long, long way away. Gradually they got louder. Penetrated the fog in her brain. Roused her to wakefulness at last. She blinked her eyes open.

An elderly man in a white coat, with a kindly face, was looking down at her. She realised she was lying in a bed, in a clinical-looking room. A nurse was standing behind the doctor.

'My dear *fraulein*, how are you feeling?'

The accent was strongly Swiss, but there was a concern in it that somehow made her throat tighten.

'What happened?' she asked weakly. 'I…I fell…'

'Yes,' agreed the kindly doctor. 'But most fortunately, although you have some injuries, none are major. However, you are not well enough to leave hospital just yet.'

'How did I get here?' Her voice was hazy.

'Mountain Rescue brought you in, summoned by Herr Petrakos. You were unconscious after falling. Now, my dear *fraulein*, you must promise me something. Our mountains are beautiful, but they can be very dangerous. You must promise me you will never try anything so reckless again.' He looked at her over the top of his glasses. 'You have been very fortunate. You have only abrasions—and your ribs are bruised, not broken. But you could have died, *fraulein*—truly, you could have died.' His voice changed, became less sombre. 'Now, we will need you to stay the night here, because we must watch for concussion. But I believe you may see Herr Petrakos—he is most anxious to see you.'

Her face closed. 'I don't want to see him.'

The doctor's eyebrows rose. 'No? But he is most concerned, *fraulein*, most concerned. Indeed, I would say he is—what is the word in English?—ah, yes—quite frantic about you.'

She could only stare. Angelos? Frantic?

'I don't want to see him,' she said again. Her voice was without expression.

The doctor looked at her questioningly a moment, then simply nodded. 'As you wish. I will let him know.'

Outside in the waiting area Angelos was pacing up and down, his face taut. When the doctor emerged, he pounced.

'She will make a full recovery,' the doctor told him immediately, and at once words in Greek broke from Angelos, relief knifing through his face. But his expression darkened at the doctor's next words.

He picked his words carefully. 'She does not wish for any visitors just now. Perhaps this afternoon,' he said, temporising, seeing Angelos's eyes flash with emotion at the refusal. 'However, Herr Petrakos…' He was picking his words even more carefully now, and Angelos stiffened. 'I think you must take pains to impress upon the *fraulein* that it is…unwise…to attempt any form of mountain-walking if there is any alcohol in the system. Even from the night before.'

Angelos's brows snapped together. *'Alcohol?'* His voice was disbelieving. 'She doesn't drink alcohol!

The doctor's eyebrows rose. 'Indeed? And yet her blood shows its presence…'

'Impossible,' said Angelos curtly. Then, abruptly, memory stabbed. He'd taken the cognac glass out of her hand...

But she couldn't possibly have drunk cognac? Why? Why would she do such a thing?

Emotion knifed in him again. There was so much he'd thought impossible about her...

His hands clenched, fighting for calm. For sense. For comprehension.

'I have to see her—it's imperative, absolutely imperative!'

But the doctor remained adamant, and seething with frustration—so much more than frustration!—Angelos could only return to the chalet. His thoughts were dark and turbid, and after he had interviewed Franz and Johann were like snakes writhing inside him.

Apfelwein—that was what she had drunk last night. Not *apfelsaft*, innocuous, harmless, apple juice, but an alcoholic drink. *Surely to God she would have noticed the difference?*

But would she—could she? If she never drank wine, or even cider, could she have known at all that it was alcoholic? Cold ran through him. Cold—and more than cold.

He walked out on to the terrace, hands gripping the wooden balcony in a death-grip.

She was intoxicated, and I didn't notice.

Memory jarred again. She'd been sipping at the cognac with half a litre of apfelwein *inside her, never having touched alcohol in her life! Heightening her intoxication. She wouldn't even have known...*

Only felt its effects…

His hands clenched again over the wooden balustrade, whitening his fingers.

I have to speak to her.

His face was stark. Grim.

Grimmer still when, the moment his untouched lunch had been cleared away, he phoned the clinic to say he was on his way down again, and that this time he would not be balked of seeing her—only to be informed, politely and regretfully by the clinic receptionist, that against all medical advice the English *fraulein* had discharged herself and gone.

The taxi drew up outside the block of flats and Thea climbed out. Despite the humid heat, she felt cold. Cold in her bones. Her very being. The rail journey from Switzerland seemed to have taken for ever, but it had not been long enough for her to shed the bleakness that engulfed her.

She had thought Angelos could do no worse to her—but she had been wrong. He had had one final, ultimate destruction for her...

She felt her shoulders sag, weariness of spirit crush her down. She closed her eyes a moment, then took a breath, forcing her shoulders back. How many times had she done that in her life? Ever since, as Kat, she'd faced the destiny she'd been slipping towards and made the transforming decision not to go that way. Not to become the person her mother had been, her mother's mother. To break that crushing chain of self-destruction dragging her down. To make something of herself, whatever it cost her.

And now she must pay another price.

Pain ripped at her, and its bitterly familiar twin—shame. Shame that she had been so un-forgivably stupid as to forget so rashly, so blindly, just what he was to her. Her nemesis—now as he had always been. Angelos Petrakos.

As she opened the entrance door of the block memory jumped in her mind. That evening when his bodyguard had stepped up, manoeuvring her

inside, admitting his employer at well. She gave
another shiver. A shudder.

Nemesis, indeed.

But she knew that then she had been fuelled
by fury, rushing through her like a tide of adrenaline—determined, driven to defeat Angelos
Petrakos, to show him that he could not destroy
her, that she would defy his destruction!

This time bleakness lapped about her. This time
it was different. She could hate Angelos all she
wanted, but he was not the cause of her down-
fall—she herself was. She and she alone had let
him do it—had been his accomplice, his conspira-
tor. It was herself she hated now, with a drear,
bleak loathing that dragged at her like weights
around her body—her treacherous, betraying
body.

Wearily, she stepped into the lift, feeling the
heat increase in the airless compartment. Again
memory stabbed at her. That crowded lift in Angelos's hotel in London, being jostled back against
him, so that her body had tensed like steel. And
as she'd gained his suite she'd turned on him.

'Don't touch me—don't ever touch me!'

Her face contorted. *Fool!* That was what had
set in motion this whole nightmare. Giving him

orders. She, Kat Jones, had presumed to dare to give the mighty Angelos Petrakos orders! To forbid him something—demand respect for herself!

She had doomed herself from that moment onwards. Because from that moment onwards, Angelos Petrakos had had only one malign aim, one fell purpose—to bring her down, to humble her, prove she could not defy him and get away with it. So, from that moment onwards, he had sought to demonstrate the futility of her presumption in denying what he, with calculated design, day by day lulling her, after all he'd done to her, from enmity to susceptibility, had determined on achieving—a seduction so skilful she had been pitifully, pathetically, incapable of realising was happening.

Until it had been too late, and Angelos Petrakos, his destruction of her complete, had forced her to see the truth about herself.

That she had yielded, of her own free will, to his most malign one….

As she let herself into her flat, that she had last left what seemed like a lifetime ago now, she felt the familiar ripping pain tear through her. She made herself ignore it, as she had made herself

ignore it all the way on her desolate journey, made
herself go through the necessary routine of turning on the air-conditioning to cool the stifling
flat, set the water to heat for a shower to refresh
her weary body, if not her even wearier spirit,
then carry the shopping she had bought on her
way home from the station, into the kitchen. She
would unpack them, make herself some tea, have a
shower, eat something—anything, she didn't care,
had no appetite—then afterwards, for the rest of
the endless, empty evening stretching ahead of
her, perhaps there was something on TV she could
watch, to blot up her thoughts. Perhaps she could
watch TV for the next month. The next year. The
rest of her life…

The ripping pain came again, and again she
stood, eyes shut, until she had fought it off. Then,
bleak depression pressing down like weights upon
her, she went to draw the curtains against the
growing dusk. Outside, the London street below
was busy—people coming and going, living their
lives, so remote from hers. A car slipped silently
along the roadway, sleek and dark and black, heading for the Opera House. For a moment memory
plucked at her and she recalled how she'd thought

the same of a similar car just before Angelos's bodyguard had hustled her inside this block.

A lifetime ago...

She let out her breath, dragging the curtains across, then headed for her bedroom, forcing herself to stay upright instead of sinking down on the bed and seeking the pointless oblivion of sleep. Long-held discipline kicked in. Doing what she didn't want to do because she had to do it. Within twenty minutes she'd unpacked, put away the groceries, made herself a cup of tea, and was standing under the shower, hot and stinging, its needles drumming on her shoulders. When she got out, she wrapped herself swiftly in her towelling dressing gown. She did not like to see her naked body.

It bore the invisible mark of shame upon it, blazoned on every curve, every centimetre of bare flesh.

She tugged the belt tighter, then unclipped her hair, reaching for a brush to pull through it and release any knots and tangles. She shook her head, feeling the fall of hair tumbling down her back. It felt long and loose and lush, like a silky cloud about her head. The pain came again, jagging at her nerves, making her head bow under the blow.

With a ragged inhalation she walked out of the bathroom, out of the bedroom, into her living room.

And stopped dead.

Angelos Petrakos was sitting on her sofa.

CHAPTER TEN

HE DIDN'T move.

Nor did she. Shock had paralysed her. Shock and something more—something even more paralysing that froze the breath in her lungs even as it made the beat of her heart jolt as if a lightning bolt had struck it.

He was sitting there just as he had before, a lifetime ago—invading her life again, taking it over, seeking to destroy it.

She swayed. *I can't, I can't go through this again, I can't, I haven't the strength...*

But she had to find that strength—had to. Had to find the strength to fight him. She waited for her anger to kick in, as it always did, giving her the strength to fight him, as it always did. But anger did not come. Only that other emotion that swept through her—terrifying her.

No! She couldn't let herself feel that—she had to control it, subdue it. Crush it back down with steel, with ice, with cold, stinging words.

'How the *hell*,' she demanded, 'did *you* get in?'

'I had your keys copied while you were in Switzerland,' he said.

His voice was clipped, impatient, as though her question was irrelevant and his answer nothing untoward. His jawline was taut, as though under tension. His whole body the same. She could see a muscle working in his cheek, his eyes like steel. Angelos Petrakos was angry.

But so what if he was? He was always angry with her...

For a moment so brief it might not have existed she felt her throat catch. Then the catch was gone, leaving only the emotion she had always felt about Angelos Petrakos.

Anger. Anger to match his.

He was speaking again, still in that same clipped, demanding voice.

'I have to speak to you—and I need answers!'

With a lithe, fluid movement he got to his feet. The suddenness made her start, and she stepped back. Then hated herself for the gesture of retreat. She would *not* retreat from him—she would stand her ground.

Yet her heart was beating like a trapped bird, her newly showered skin was damp and clammy.

Though her towelling robe was thick and fleecy, she was burningly conscious of her bare body beneath.

Memory stabbed again, coming between the defences she kept against it, driven through by the presence of the man standing there.

Madness possessed her just for a moment—an instant of madness, of wanting to hurl herself at him, to throw herself into his arms and feel them wrap around her, holding her, folding her close against him, cradling her face and lifting her mouth to his…

She felt faint with it— faint with the knowledge that it could never happen. Angelos Petrakos would never touch her again. Never in all her life.

She waited for the feeling of relief that thought must bring—but it did not come.

Why doesn't it come? Why don't I feel the relief I should feel—must feel!—knowing that Angelos will never touch me again?

'Why did you go before I could speak to you?'

His words, harsh and grating, cut through her torment. Her eyes widened disbelievingly.

'You expected me to stay?' A rough, scornful laugh rasped in her throat, tearing past the vocal cords that had contracted painfully. 'My God, you really thought that? You underestimate how good a teacher you are, Angelos! You taught me well—taught me everything I need to know about you! Taught me that when you want to destroy me you do it—whatever the method is.' She had to force the words out now, her throat tighter than a drum. 'Even the one you used this time.' Her voice dropped and she swallowed, as if a stone were blocking her lungs. But she made herself say the words—the words he had said to her in his moment of triumph. 'Showing me the truth about myself...'

Dark light flashed in his eyes. 'Truth? Don't use that word to me—' Greek broke from him, vehement and harsh. A hand slashed through the air and she flinched. 'You nearly *died* that morning! Refusing to take my hand even to save your own life!'

She stepped towards him, hands clenching, face contorted. 'Take *your* hand? Take your hand? After what you'd done to me?'

His expression changed. Color drained from his face, leaving it stark and gaunt.

'I didn't know,' he said. His voice was stiff, dragging, as if he didn't want to say what he was saying. 'I had no idea—none.' His eyes met hers, with that same reluctance in them. 'I had no idea you'd been served alcohol at dinner.'

She stared blankly. Not understanding.

A brief, humourless laugh came from him as he enlightened her, his voice still harsh.

'You didn't realise? But why should you? You have no idea of the effects of alcohol, have you? No idea how it can…lower resistance to temptation.' His eyes rested on her. He inhaled sharply. 'You drank *apfelwein*—apple wine. Not *apfelsaft*—apple juice—that night. Johann served you, and he didn't know you never drink alcohol. And you—you didn't know the difference because you've never tasted alcohol, have you? And then I saw you inhaling my cognac fumes. Did you try drinking any of that as well?' He saw her expression and nodded. '*Thee mou!* Cognac—neat spirits—on top of wine, and your system totally unused to alcohol! No wonder you—'

He stopped. Took another sharp, razored inhalation, his eyes boring into hers like spears. Knives were slashing inside him. They had been at work since he'd been told she'd walked out of the clinic and, all the time since then, waiting to hear from his security staff the moment, the *moment* she appeared at her flat again, as he had been counting on her to do. And now—finally—she was here, and he was—finally!—confronting her with the truth.

The truth he'd discovered far too late…

She was staring at him. Her face was without expression, her voice without expression as she finished the sentence for him.

'No wonder I came on to you the way I did.'

Angelos's voice was heavy, forced from him. 'If I had known, I would not have touched you.'

She looked at him, her eyes withering. 'No— you'd have saved it, wouldn't you? You wouldn't want me to have the excuse that I was drunk when I fell into bed with you!' Her mind was in a tumult, emotions scything inside her head—what Angelos had done to her, what she had let him do, and, pouring in over the top of that, what his disclosure had done to her. Words blurted from her, anguished and tormented. 'But you've won more than you ever dreamt!'

His brows snapped together. 'Won?'

She gave a high, demented laugh, eyes wild. 'Yes! Your triumph is even greater than you know! You wanted me back in the gutter, back down in the pit I'd crawled out of, and now you can boast you've done it again! You've proved everything you could possibly want to prove! That I can never, never escape my past—never escape!' Bitterness scoured her mouth. 'I'm like my mother, and her mother before her! As weak as they were! Self-indulgent and self-destructive!'

'What are you talking about?' Angelos demanded. He took a step towards her, but she lurched backwards.

'You didn't know, did you?' Her eyes were blazing with loathing, but it was not for him alone. 'My God, you missed a trick there! You could have threatened me with so much more than you did! Threatened to expose me to Giles for even more than what I did to you as Kat!' Her words were vicious, stinging like hornets. 'My mother was a junkie, my grandmother an alcoholic!'

He stilled. 'That's why you never drink.' It was not a question. It was a statement.

'I wasn't going to go their way—I was *never* going to go their way!' Her voice was low and bitter, and filled with loathing. Loathing for her mother's weakness, her grandmother's weakness. Her own weakness. Her own deadly, fatal weakness that had brought her to this pass.

He held up a hand. 'Two glasses of wine and a taste of cognac does not make you an alcoholic!'

'No,' she answered. 'It makes me a fool...' Self-loathing choked her. 'A fool,' she repeated, ex-coriation in her voice. 'A fool who let you show me the truth about myself—that I was too weak to resist you even after everything you'd done to me. That my stupid, pathetic protest to you, claim-ing that I couldn't bear for you to touch me, was just empty bravado! You *knew* you could prove otherwise! You knew for five years! Ever since I stood there in your hotel suite and let you help yourself to me, kiss me and touch me and call me a *whore*!'

Her chest was heaving, breath like razors in her lungs, eyes distended as she was emptied, silenced.

Angelos stood there quite motionless, only the muscle above his cheekbone working.

'But you weren't, were you?' he said. There was nothing in his voice, nothing at all. As if that were the only way his words would come. 'Because how could you have been a whore, Kat, five years ago—when you were a virgin?'

The silence was absolute. She closed her eyes, then opened them again. He was speaking again, and still there was nothing in his voice.

'When you left my bed to escape me I saw the

evidence. I didn't want to believe it—how I didn't want to believe it—but it's the truth, isn't it? *Isn't it?*'

He saw the answer in her eyes, and now his voice was harsh as he went on.

'So hearing me denounce you like that in my hotel suite five years ago made you angry. Your temper got the better of you and you took my watch to get back at me, out of furious pique.'

Thea's breath incised her, eyes lashed at him. 'My God, you conceited fool!' she spat. 'You think I acted out of *pique*? When out in the street was—'

She stopped. Cold iced around her as memory hit. The terror that had possessed her, the shaking desperation.

In the total silence Angelos's eyes were suddenly alert. Super-focussed. Trapping her in a beam of laser light.

Then he spoke.

'Go on, Kat,' he said. His voice was measured, but with a note in it that curdled her. '"When out in the street was…"?'

She wouldn't answer. Couldn't. Heard again the sick, twisted words that Mike had spoken to her so long ago.

'Tell me, Kat.' Angelos's voice pulled her back to the present. 'Why did you steal from me? Not out of temper and pique—so why? What made you risk breaking the law, a gaol sentence—worse?' His mouth twisted. 'My anger at you?'

Her face contorted. Words broke from her. 'I was desperate, that's why! I needed money, that's why! That's why I came to your suite! That's why I *crawled* to you, grovelled to you and begged you to give me back that job you'd taken away on a bloody whim! Because I needed money! Money the job would pay me—money I could give to a sick psycho so he wouldn't take his razor to me! He was waiting for me downstairs, on the street outside the hotel, and I had to give him *something*. Either the promise of a lucrative job so I could use the money to pay him with—or something else. Anything else! Anything that would have placated him—bought me time! Kept his razor off my face!'

For an endless moment there was complete silence. Then she began to shake.

Slowly, as if her arms weighed heavy like lead, she wrapped them around her body, as if to hold herself upright. Angelos stepped forward. His hands closed around her arms as they bound her.

Words came from his mouth, but she did not understand them. Then he spoke again, in English this time. His voice was controlled. Very, very controlled.

'Who was this, Kat? Who was threatening you?'

She spoke through gritted teeth, a throat that would hardly let breath pass. Her eyes stared past Angelos, back into the past.

'His name was Mike, and he was a photographer. He was always creepy, but a friend persuaded me to let him do my first model portfolio. What he wanted…' her voice shook a moment '…was to take porn shots—and to pimp me to other men. If didn't co-operate he…he…threatened to cut my face. I knew he would carry out his threat.' She swallowed. It was like swallowing glass. 'Because he'd already cut my friend—scarred her for life, to punish her. So—so I had to buy him off. It was all I could do. I needed that job you'd offered me. It would have paid me enough money to keep him happy for a while. When you kicked me off the shoot I came to you to beg for it back. When you refused, I panicked—I stole your watch. It was something—anything—to give to Mike, waiting outside on his motorbike. I knew it would be worth a few thousand—it must be, or a rich man like you wouldn't wear it. It would keep Mike happy. Buy me time.'

She stopped talking. There was silence. Only the dim noise of the cars outside on the street below.

Angelos's grip around her arms was like steel. 'What happened when you left the police station? Did he find you?' There was no emotion in his voice. Only the question.

There was none in hers as she answered him. She could not look at him, only stare beyond him at the far wall. Into the past.

'No. He was dead. He smashed his bike into a brick wall, following me down to the police station when I was arrested. I heard a traffic cop telling the desk sergeant. I saw the photo on his driving licence.' She was silent. Then, 'So it was all for nothing. I stole from you for nothing. I tried to save my skin, knowing that with Mike dead it was the law I had to fear having stolen. So I lied my way out of being charged with theft. And then...' Her voice hollowed. 'Then I discovered there was still something else to fear—your vengeance. Destroying everything I'd made of myself. Pushing me back into the pit I'd climbed out of. Leaving me with nothing. All over again.'

Silence stretched between them. Unbridgeable. Angelos's hands fell from her and she felt herself sway, as though he had been keeping her upright. Then, slowly, as if forcing himself, he spoke.

'Why did you never tell me this?'

Now she looked at him. His face was stark, etched from stone.

Her voice sliced with scorn. 'What possible reason would I have for thinking you could be moved by pathetic pleas from *me*? I'd already begged you to give me back the job you'd taken from me—hiring me one day and chucking me away the next! What would you have cared about a psycho out to get me?'

The expression in his face changed. 'Do you not know why,' he asked slowly, his eyes never leaving hers, 'I dropped you from the campaign?'

She turned away, shrugging, breaking eye contact. It disturbed her.

'I was too mouthy. Too common. A street rat— just as you called me when you stopped me marrying Giles.'

'None of those things. I dropped you, Kat, for the same reason I took you to Switzerland.'

She rounded on him. 'I *know* why you took me there! So you could throw it in my face, rub my nose in it, that you could make me want you! And you did,' she finished bitterly.

'Just as,' he replied, *'you'd* made me want *you* five years ago.' His mouth twisted. 'You were like no other female I'd ever met. Oh, not just that incredible body and that face of yours—that beauty you wear as carelessly as if you didn't know you had it! But the woman behind the beauty. The one with the attitude, the raw edginess, the beautiful, insolent mouth that answered me back, that made me think there was only one way to silence it. *That's* why I dropped you from that campaign.'

His eyes were branding her, boring into her.

'I didn't want a woman like that in a publicity campaign for one of my businesses.' His eyes held hers for one moment longer. 'I wanted her in my bed.' He took a sharp, indrawn breath. 'But I never mix business with pleasure, Kat. I never let the women I take to my bed use me for their careers. *Never.* So I knew that if I wanted you for myself I could not let you do that shoot. When I made my decision to make my relationship with you personal, not professional, I countermanded my instructions to my campaign director. He'd already notified your agency of my first decision, and so had to issue a cancellation. I was going to contact you the following day, and tell you, but you,' his voice turned into a blade, 'pre-empted me by arriving at my suite that same evening. Offering me your body to get the job back.' Now the blade of his voice was cutting his own flesh. 'I did not realize how desperate you had cause to be. I only knew that I was angry, so very angry with you, because you'd made it impossible for me to have an affair with you by showing me how you would try and use it to advance your career.'

There was contempt in his voice, but it was not for her.

She was staring at him. 'I *never*,' she said slowly, each word biting, '*never* offered myself to you! You accused me of it, but I never did. I never would.' She took a painful scissoring breath. 'I told you my mother was a junkie, my grand-mother an alcoholic.' She looked at him. Looked at him unflinchingly. 'How do you think they funded their addictions?' She paused. 'They were prostitutes—both of them. Raised in care, like I was. And when I discovered that about them—I vowed I would never be like them! So I started to make something of myself—started modelling, because there was nothing else I was qualified to do. But I never touched a drop of alcohol, or touched drugs of any kind, and I never, *ever* let sex anywhere near me. *Never!* Until—'

She stopped, shame flooding through her like a drowning tide. Shame like she had felt when she had stolen from him. But then she'd had desperation, terror, to fuel her theft. What had fuelled her into falling into Angelos's arms, his bed, that night in Switzerland?

He gave her the answer himself.

'Until you drank wine and cognac and it washed away your guard.' His eyes shadowed. 'It was the only way you'd succumb to me.' He turned away, walking across to the window, pulling back the curtain halfway to stare down into the street. The car he'd arrived in, black and sleek, was hovering by the kerb. He would go down to it, drive away, leave her. Get out of her life for ever. Free her from the curse he had been to her…

He heard his own voice echoing in his head.

The mountains expose the truth…

The words mocked him like a whip on bleeding skin. He'd thought he'd expose the truth about her—find whether she had truly changed from the woman she had been five years ago. But she had never been that woman…

He'd known nothing about her. The woman who

had walked the mountains with him, at his side, remained as hidden from him as she had always been. He thought of the life she'd had—growing up with the bleak, damning knowledge of her background, her determination to break free of it. He thought of how that life had tried to suck her back into its fetid, filthy pit when some foul, psychotic scum had threatened her, and what she'd done to try and save herself.

What it had cost her to do so.

He heard his voice speaking to her as if from very far away.

'I ruined you. When you stole from me I ruined you without knowing why you'd done what you had—what had driven you to do it. Ruined you because I presumed you had come to me to sell your body. Ruined you in my anger and my arrogance. And then I ruined you all over again when I saw you with a man you wanted to marry—a man who would have given you security and a place in the world, a place you'd earned. Despite what I did to you, you made yourself get up off the floor again, when I'd thrown you down on to it, and you remade yourself as Thea.'

He shifted his weight, moving his shoulders as if the tension in them had become unbearable.

'And in Switzerland…' His voice was harsher now, serrated. 'My arrogance triumphed yet again. I wanted to test whether you had indeed remade yourself—turned yourself from Kat to Thea, turned your back on all that Kat had been, paid your dues for all that she had done. And—' he took a harsh, ragged inhalation of breath '—above all I wanted to force you to admit the truth. The truth I'd known for so long, for five long years, since I first met you. The truth you'd denied, hurling defiance at me, forbidding me to touch you, lying that you could not bear it…could not bear my touch! It became my whole aim to keep you with me, to disarm you day by day, get you to lower that fierce, ferocious guard against me, get you to trust me—get you to admit your desire for me. The desire I knew with absolute certainty you felt but would not admit.'

His eyes were veiled again, lashes dipping over their obsidian depths. 'And you did—I achieved my goal, triumphed in it. But I didn't know.' His voice changed again, and the contempt in it was naked—contempt for himself. 'I didn't know I had achieved it only because you were intoxicated that night—so intoxicated you yielded to me what you have guarded so long. Your virginity. And when you had, you hated me so much for what I'd done to you that you fled from me and would have rather risked your life than take my hand to save you. Because of everything I'd done to you for so, so long...'

He shook his head slowly, from side to side, as if he would negate everything he'd said. But how could he? Arrogance and anger had driven him for five years—and they had brought him here now. With everything he'd come to want in ashes at his feet. Burned by his own anger, his own arrogance.

He fell silent. The silence stretched between them.

Thoughts flowed into Thea's head. Thoughts that should not be there. Emotions that should not be there.

He lifted his eyes to her.

'I should ask your forgiveness, but how could you forgive me? How could anything I do make up for what I put you through?' He took a ragged breath. 'Go back to your Honourable Giles, Thea. Tell him that I threatened you and blackmailed you and behaved unforgivably to you. Go back and find your happiness.'

She swallowed, eyes shifting away, then back

to him. The thoughts that should not be there, the emotions that should not be there, were still there.

She spoke, her voice low and difficult. 'He's marrying someone else. A family friend. I saw the announcement in a newspaper at Dover. She's very suitable. Far more than me. I didn't love him—I was only fond of him. That isn't a reason to marry someone. It would have been wrong of me to marry him. But I wanted what you said I wanted—security, a place to belong.' She looked away again for a moment. 'I had no family—not any that I wanted—that anyone would want! So I wanted to marry someone who did. Giles knows all his ancestors, over hundreds of years—it was unimaginable to me. I didn't want his title, or his country house, or his wealth. I wanted his family—his ancestors. Because I had none. That's why I should never have agreed to marry him.' She paused, then made herself go on. 'And though I hated you for forcing me to see what I was doing I *was* lying to him about myself—about being Kat, deceiving him just as you accused me of doing.'

It was hard to say it, but she had to. It was true. As true as the other truth she was shielding from her head. The truth that Angelos Petrakos had forced her to face.

The final truth about herself.

The one that she could not deny. The one that had nothing to do with whether she had drunk wine that night in the mountain chalet, or whether she had been a virgin when she'd given herself to him, or with anything of the bitter past between them, the anger and the hatred.

The truth had been inside her since she had fled from Switzerland, and could not be denied. It was here now, as she stood looking at him—the truth that would last all her life.

But to what purpose?

Anguish crushed her.

She had discovered a truth in Angelos's arms that she could never deny. But it was a hopeless truth—a truth that could only mock her...

To have come through so much! To have taken so long a journey, for so many years, through such hardships, such anguish and anger and bitterness, and find such a truth at the end of it!

There was a burning behind her eyelids. Hot and painful. She tried to keep her eyes closed, to quench the burning, but it would not be quenched. She could feel the burning liquefy, like molten fire, feel it squeeze past her eyelids, hot on her cheeks.

She heard him draw breath, speak—words she didn't know. Then there were footsteps—rapid, heavy. Then his presence, tangible, in front of her.

And then his finger brushed the burning molten tears.

'Thea—my Thea—'

His voice sounded broken, which was strange— so strange. So strange, too, the brush of his fingertip on one cheek and then the other. And stranger still the cupping of her chin, the tilting of her face up to him.

'Don't cry! I've hurt and harmed you so much! So much I cannot bear to think of it! When I saw you fall, slipping down the rockface, risking death rather than take my outstretched hand, I felt a horror I have never felt—never want to feel again in all my life.'

His voice was low, intense, his body so close to hers. Though her eyes were still screwed so tight shut she could feel his presence, his heat. His height and his breadth and the scent of his body. The warmth of his breath. His hands cupping her face, thumbs smoothing away the hot, molten tears slipping silently down her cheeks.

'I ask for nothing—nothing. Least of all your forgiveness for what I have done. I deserve nothing from you—only your hatred for all I have done! But I beg you, from my heart, to believe me now when I say to you that the night you gave yourself to me I meant you no harm, no ill intent. Though you have every reason to think I did. That night, those days we were together, will be a treasure to me all my life. They showed me a truth about myself that I will carry to my grave—and you hold it in your hands, worthless though it can be to you. It is all that I can offer. My heart, my love—'

His eyes were gazing down into hers, ablaze, but her vision was blurred with tears. There was a ball of pain within her, squeezing tight, so tight...

He was speaking still, his voice shaken and vehement. 'I have been monstrous to you—but I will beg forgiveness all my days. Don't cry, my Thea, don't cry. I will not let you cry. So brave, so beautiful, and I love you so much—so very much!'

She was crying more, tears pouring from her, and with an oath he wrapped her to him, folded her against his body, cradled her and rocked her, his hand soothing on her hair, his arm tight around her waist, her face buried in his shoulder.

How long she cried she did not know. Five years of tears. A long, long time to cry.

He scooped her up, lowered them both down upon the sofa, and went on holding her, letting her weep, soothing her, kissing her hair, rocking her gently, murmuring to her in Greek, in English, all the things he had never said to her but which came from him now.

She stilled at last, no tears left in her, but he held her still, exhausted, drained, cradled across his lap. He kissed her eyelids.

'My Thea,' he said again.

She opened her eyes. Opened her eyes to see his, the truth pouring into her.

'Is it true?' Her voice was a whisper, her fingers clutching at his lapel.

He gave a smile. Crooked, unsure. Unsure of *her*.

'True that I love you? Oh, yes...' He took a ragged breath, his eyes questioning. Fearful of her answer lest it destroy him. 'I loved you the night I made love to you—you whom I had desired for so long, who had become more to me, though I scarcely realised it, than any woman I had known.

I loved you as I made love to you—though I did not have the words for it, only the emotion, though it was unrecognisable to me, having never felt it before. I only knew that I wanted to keep you with me from then on, never part with you.'

His voice changed, grew haunted. 'But in the morning you were gone—and when I realised, saw the evidence of what I had done to you— taken your virginity, all unknowing—then I knew why you had fled from me, knew I had to find you. And when I did...' Again his voice changed, tearing at his throat. 'When I did—you risked death rather than letting me save you...' He gave a shuddering breath. 'So I know I can ask nothing from you.'

'You have it, all the same,' she said. Her voice was rich—rich with promise, with revelation. Her fingers tightened on his lapel as she gazed up at him. How could this be? she wondered. Moments ago she had stood accepting the devastation of the truth of what she felt, the revelation of her own heart, and thought only that it must mock her all her life. And now—

'I love you,' she told him. It was all she had to say—all he needed to hear.

He crushed her to him, holding her so close

against him that she could scarcely breathe, but joy blazed through her. She loved him—and was loved.

'How can that be?' she whispered.

He kissed her softly, tenderly. With all his heart. 'Can you forgive me what I did to you?'

Again the note of doubt, of disbelief was there.

'You didn't know, and I didn't tell you why I wanted that job so desperately. And Angelos—' She laid a finger on his mouth. As he would have spoken, her eyes troubled. 'I did steal from you. I can't deny that. And whether my fear and desperation were enough to justify it, I can't answer—I daren't answer!'

'You've been through so much—all your life.' His voice was ragged. 'Faced so much, overcome so much, achieved so much. As Kat, as Thea— your courage, your determination, your integrity, shine from you! Dear God, how much I love you!' He kissed her again hungrily, urgently, possessively.

And beneath his lips hers opened to him, desire lighting in her like a flame, kindling and quickening as she wound her hands around his neck, clung to his lean, strong body.

He swept her up, striding across the room, carrying her into the bedroom, lowering her down upon the bed's wide, waiting surface.

'Are you sure? Are you truly sure this is what you want?'

He had asked her the question before, but this time his fate hung upon it.

She gazed up at him. In her eyes a smile gleamed. Warming his heart.

'Oh, yes,' she breathed. 'Oh, yes—my own, adored Angelos.' She opened her arms wide to him and as he came down beside her she clung to him, whispered in his ear. 'And not a single drop of any intoxicant but one.' Her eyes softened, and she hugged him tight against her. 'Love,' she said. 'Pure and potent love...'

He gave a low, soft laugh—and then there was no more need for words.

Only love, made whole, and pure, and everlasting.

Thea lay warm and nestled against Angelos. Happiness, as unbelievable as it was radiant, enwrapped her as closely as his strong arms wound about her. She gazed into his eyes as they returned her gaze, love light in them both.

She lifted a hand to touch his face.

'How can this be?' she asked wonderingly. 'How can such happiness be?'

He smiled down at her. Tenderness and love filled his gaze. 'I only know I don't deserve it—not after all I did to you.

She laid a finger across his mouth. 'No—it's over now, all that bitter past between us. I won't let it haunt you.'

'I'll spend my life making you happy, trying to undo what I did.'

'It's gone, Angelos—truly, it's gone. And now we have this…' The note of wonder was back in her voice.

It was in her heart, too, alongside the radiance of her happiness. How strange life was, she thought, that out of all the anger and bitterness love should have flowered.

When had it started to blossom? she wondered. Oh, she had long felt the power Angelos had over her—not the malign power he had wielded, but that overwhelming male power that drew her eye endlessly to him, that made her quiver with awareness of his presence, awakening her nascent female instincts—but it had taken the lonely beauty of the mountains they had shared, those firelit evenings together for her to start to see him as a person other than the forbidding, distant stranger who had so persecuted her.

And then, in the ecstasy of his arms, it had blazed to life, possessing her even as he had possessed her body and she had given herself to him.

A shadow passed over her eyes.

'If I hadn't run from your bed that morning—'

His arms tightened around her as he heard the distress in her voice. 'If I had given you reason to trust me, you would not have fled,' he told her. He kissed her gently, soothing her. 'My beloved Thea,' he murmured.

The shadow in her eyes glinted into a smile. 'So I am Thea now, finally?'

His eyes smiled in return, but his voice as he answered was sombre. 'But you are Kat, too—Kat who overcame what she had been born to, who had more courage and guts in her little finger than I have in my whole body and made something of herself from the nothing she was born with. And then made herself Thea after all I did to her...'

Her eyes glinted again, seeking to draw him away from dark memories that were not needed now, nor ever would be again now that all had been healed by love.

'Kat was very lippy, though,' she murmured.

Now, at last, his mouth curved into a reminiscent smile. 'Oh, she was indeed,' he agreed. 'But I have to admit,' he mused, 'that was part of your charm...'

'Novelty value? After all those flunkeys kowtowing to you?' she probed wickedly.

'Very possibly,' he said dryly. 'But,' he went on—and his voice had changed, was serious now—'Kat stood up for herself, and so did Thea. Whatever I threw at them.'

Again she laid a finger across his mouth. 'No—the past is over.'

He caught her finger with his lips and kissed it, and then kissed her mouth.

'Only the future matters now,' he told her, and cradled her yet closer against him. But though his arms were strong about her, his voice, when he spoke again, was uncertain—hesitant. 'Your name is yours, and yours alone to choose, but...' He paused, then took an indrawn breath.

Thea could see the sudden tension in his face, the uncertain wariness in his eyes.

'Would you consider,' he went on, 'taking another name? Would you consider taking the name Mrs Angelos Petrakos?'

She stilled, looking up at him. Then, out of no-where, his features blurred.

His head dipped to hers, his mouth to hers.

She clung to his mouth, her hands winding up around his neck, holding him to her.

'It's a *wonderful* name,' she said. 'The best I could ever have!'

He pulled back from her a fraction, love blazing from him. For a moment they only gazed at each other. Then words were no longer necessary.

EPILOGUE

MRS ANGELOS PETRAKOS stood at the rail of the deck and glanced up at her husband. Love turned over in her heart. Angelos smiled down at her. The sea breeze ruffled his hair, and the rays of the setting sun bronzed his skin. Before them, the azure hues of the Aegean were turning molten, and the lights in the harbour on the distant shore were gleaming in the growing dusk. Warmth enveloped her—and not just the warmth of the Greek summer.

The soft chug of the yacht's engine sent a low vibration through the hull as the boat made its slow way along the coastline.

'Are you sure you want such a remote honeymoon?' Angelos asked her. 'We could easily put into port, if you prefer.'

Thea smiled. 'I think your private island sounds idyllic,' she told him.

'I hope you like it,' he said, that note of uncertainty still in his voice.

'I like anywhere that you are,' she said, and leant against him, feeling the lean strength of his body supporting her.

She lifted her glass of champagne to her lips, and Angelos did likewise.

'Drink it slowly,' he advised her. 'It's heady stuff.'

She laughed. 'I will. I'm still very, very cautious about alcohol. But I do think—' her eyes gleamed '—that on my wedding day I should risk a glass of champagne.'

He bent to kiss her. 'And perhaps for breakfast tomorrow?'

Thea shook her head. 'Orange juice,' she said firmly.

He smiled fondly. 'Then orange juice it shall be. Everything in the world that you want that is in my power, shall be.'

Her eyes lit with emotion. 'Oh, my darling Angelos—I have very simple needs. I need only one thing in my life, now and for ever.' She paused, fighting the sudden tightening of her throat. So much anger and bitterness and hatred and tears had gone by, and now all that dark past was over— truly over. Her life was beginning again—anew, afresh—and at her side was all she wanted. All she would ever want.

'I only need you…' she said.

He raised his glass to her. 'You have me for ever,' he promised her. 'And my love for all eternity.'

'And you have mine,' she vowed.

She touched his glass with hers, and they drank a toast to each other, to their love together. A long, deep sigh escaped her, rich with happiness. Angelos's arm wrapped around her shoulder and they stood, side by side, gazing out across the sea towards their future together.

* * * * *